The Story of the Madman

DISCARD

CARAF Books

———

Caribbean and African Literature
Translated from French

Carrol F. Coates, Editor

Clarisse Zimra, J. Michael Dash, John Conteh-Morgan,
and Elisabeth Mudimbe-Boyi, Advisory Editors

The Story of the Madman

MONGO BETI

Translated by Elizabeth Darnel

Afterword by Patricia-Pia Célérier

University Press of Virginia

CHARLOTTESVILLE AND LONDON

This project is supported in part by a grant
from the National Endowment for the Arts.

Publication of this translation was assisted by a grant
from the French Ministry of Culture
Originally published in French as *L'histoire du fou*
© Éditions Julliard, 1994

THE UNIVERSITY PRESS OF VIRGINIA
Translation and afterword © 2001
by the Rector and Visitors of the University of Virginia
All rights reserved
Printed in the United States of America
First published 2001

Library of Congress Cataloging-in-Publication Data

Beti, Mongo, 1932–
   [Histoire du fou. English]
   The story of the madman / Mongo Beti ; translated by Elizabeth
Darnel ; afterword by Patricia-Pia Célérier.
      p. cm. — (Caribbean and African literature translated from French)
   ISBN 0-8139-2048-5 (cloth : alk. paper). — ISBN 0-8139-2049-3 (pbk. :
alk. paper)
      I. Darnel, Elizabeth. II. Title. III. Series.

PQ3989.2.B45 H5713 2001
843'.914—dc21

                                                          00-069339

Contents

The Story of the Madman

To my friend Gustave Massiah

In this city where, despite the large population of madmen, there is not a single asylum or hospital willing to admit them, a young man, thirty at most and as naked as they say Adam was in the garden of Eden, wanders daily through the crowded streets or, engrossed in soliloquies punctuated by sporadic and incoherent smiles, rummages mechanically in the refuse from which he gleans his food, clucking continuously. The locals recall that for a long time he wore a sooty cloak that was both rough and slimy. Nowadays, he appears everywhere, in squares where lovers daydream, on sidewalks where listless crowds bustle, and at intersections where traffic stagnates, like a living and realistic illustration in an anatomy lesson. He obstinately favors the business district and the swarming of indifferent and dapper young employees. He is tall, well built, but increasingly lean as the days go by because the fodder he garners from the garbage is meager. Sometimes, from beneath the dense and filthy hairiness, his usually dull and uncertain gaze comes alive; he shudders and scrutinizes the crowd as he used to do already so long ago, in that other city of the republic, the capital, when he would harpoon in his little brother from a sea of students —in those days he would come when school let out to wait for this child whose protection had been entrusted to him and on whom he had to report to the patriarch of a distant community of peasants while, for his part, unbeknownst to his family, he had abandoned his studies and was living off his wits among a band of prematurely emancipated adolescents.

If, perchance, some surprised passerby should stop to observe this creature, so strange a specimen and yet rendered so familiar

The Story of the Madman

by the sheer number of madmen, he will see the naked man tense for an instant as his lips tremble and whisper a futile call to this brother who used to wave his arm but who will come no more.

In this immense, but paralyzed, city, where no one works any longer and where schools lie as deserted as necropolises, it is not uncommon for swarms of squalling children to chase the naked man, not just any naked man, although the town is infested with them, but precisely this one, like some cursed creature, and when they catch him they throw stones at him; then the naked man's face may be cruelly wounded, the corners of his mouth bloodied, his eyes reddened with tears, and his gait rendered unsteady.

Sometimes passing adults gather and gaze persistently but pitilessly at the madman, as one would look at a bandit dangling at the end of a rope or at a pilloried child murderer. At times, a smile lights up the onlookers' faces, and one of them may even step forward, jostle the naked man—striking him brutally until he falls to the ground—and kick him repeatedly. And it is all the others can do not to applaud.

Such are the residents of this great port, trapped as they are in the spiral of the shadow war against the secret or visible police forces of the chief of state, while combatants from both sides fall daily, usually in anonymity and silence.

The great port's crowds are so ghastly when they want to avenge their heroes who have succumbed under torture, before the firing squad, or under the axe, that it can be safely predicted how one day soon a madman, in a senseless rage, will kill this madman.

Until that day, which will deliver him from his curse, the naked man—the madman whose usually dull gaze sometimes grows searching when he calls, in vain, his murdered brother, Zoaétoa, son of Zoaételeu, noble descendant in the thirty-second generation of the illustrious lineage of Zambo Menduga, but today the pitiful victim of a father whose innocent and rustic philosophy has caused so many misfortunes—pursues his endless wanderings.

The Story of the Madman

For the madman has a story that is all the more pitiful because it is not really his story, as you may judge for yourself, but the story of his father and, to be exact, the story of a people who dreamed much and suffered even more. It is, in fact, the story that will be told here.

So, indirectly as it were, here is the story of the madman who wandered the streets of an African city crawling with madmen and where there was not a single specialized establishment capable of receiving them.

Zoaételeu was a strapping young man of exceptional strength with a reputation for engaging in village brawls enthusiastically and to his advantage. The junior member of an impressive brood of males, he remained single for a long time because, traditionally, precedence is given to the eldest sons, out of respect for nature, which has done the same; but often, when the turns of younger brothers come, the family finds itself short of means and brides are expensive in Bantu country. This is what happened to Zoaételeu, and, consequently, the customary shiftlessness, idleness, and conventional orgies of male peasants filled the greater part of his youth.

As he approached forty and was desperately languishing in celibacy, an amazing set of circumstances brought about the sudden passing of his two elder brothers, so that, in accordance with custom, he inherited their spouses, albeit with the wives' consent, for he was truly handsome in those days—more muscular and broad-backed than a leopard crouched for a pounce.

But it was also around the time he turned forty that, through a no less amazing set of circumstances, Zoaételeu became yet another victim of absurd denunciations. This plague had caused endless devastation in the new republic ever since the promulgation of its independence on January 1, 1960, amid turmoil, discord, and bloodshed, three scourges whose evil alliance would inflict tragedy after tragedy on our people. Although there had been no precedent for it on the black continent, the republic, when it was still only a colony, had believed it could break free from the yoke by means of a revolutionary guerrilla group

The Story of the Madman

modeled on Ho Chi Minh's and General Vo Nguyen Giap's epic enterprise. Delighted finally to have the opportunity to take an easy revenge for its Asian vexations, the former colonial power threw both its political and military tactical experience into the balance: it installed an accommodating dictator and made him endorse an insidious civil war. For all the populations, this marked the start of an endless period of tears and suffering that continues still as I write these lines, and Zoaételeu's adventure is but one example among many: for a people as for a river, be it the puniest stream, any attempt to reverse its course is doomed to fail.

Independence is the factor one constantly comes back to, as if to the source of our misfortunes. In the language of Zoaételeu and his kin, which often consists of comparisons that at first glance seem preposterous, I would say that for this man independence was like death: it was impossible for him to imagine what came after it, since no one to his knowledge had ever come back. At any rate, the consequences would not be long in coming, nor would Zoaételeu dally before making a merry entrance into hell rather than to heaven as anticipated.

Having landed in the police station of the neighboring garrison town where he had strayed, God only knows how, and after receiving several truncheon blows to the head and back because he had been unable to produce his identity card upon being caught in a raid, the village idiot took a wild shot at pacifying his torturer by denouncing Zoaételeu as the strategic link in a network of clandestine militants and guerrilla fighters,* a heterogeneous group against whom the chief of state, whom the former colonial power gingerly supported, had just initiated a merciless war. That was enough for the police in those days, as it still is today, come to think of it. Uniformed men invaded the village without warning, hurled themselves on Zoaételeu, thrashing him with increasing severity as he shouted

---

*As I was able to ascertain during my investigation, this was an all-purpose formula that appeared as is in all the files concerning similar situations.—*Author's note*

more loudly that he had done nothing, that he was innocent, and that a human being should at least be told what crime he had committed before being punished.

Zoaételeu was thrown unceremoniously into a jeep and spirited off as if in a whirlwind without so much as a pause in the storm of blows under which he was submerged.

The village was petrified, as was the entire province, where similar incidents occurred here and there every day. Rumor had it that the other provinces of the republic were not exempt, with the exception of the chief of state's native province, although this rumored privilege was not corroborated by people who had traveled there.

No one ventured near the successive locales where Zoaételeu was known to be held, not even to inquire about his health or, at the very least, to demand an explanation for his arrest and for the harsh treatment to which he had been and which he was doubtless still suffering.

When Zoaételeu finally reappeared after six years that had possibly seemed more endless to his people than to himself, and as the chief of state was pursuing against the revolutionary underground forces of the West a war that grew daily more intense and that was slowly draining the resources of the nation, it was immediately obvious that he was a changed man, physically at any rate. His once muscular arms, as large and compact as the trunk of a young banana tree, had withered; the once plump and venous flesh of his calves had melted, had puckered somehow. He was now a debilitated old man who, due to a fracture of the spine resulting from his cruel prison treatment, walked somewhat asymmetrically, with an irregular gait and a twisted carriage. Unwittingly he had become the pathetic illustration of our collective misfortune.

He usually abstained from dwelling on the tribulations of what he modestly called his exile; for him to do so, he had to be drunk, or at least to be on the verge of inebriation. Then, indignant and yet confused, he would embark on the tale of his misfortunes, angrily calling down the thunderbolts of immanent justice on his torturers.

He was now as adamantly affable and peace-loving as he had been avid for brawls in his youth. No longer fit for physical exertion, and all the less for work, he spent entire days seated on the threshold of his house, as patriarchs are wont to do, observing people as if he were discovering the world and formulating serene remarks on life that earned him the reputation of a wise man and delighted his ever dense ranks of assiduous visitors.

As a result, mature men hastened from neighboring clans to offer him their daughters. He, who had been single for so long, soon found himself at the head of a vast tribe, for which he bore a passion that, with increasing frequency through the years, came to be considered excessive, even by his own relatives.

When I met him in 198 . . . , I was, like those tourists primed on images and tales fabricated and publicized by western professionals of exotica, exceedingly sensitive to the ridiculous aspect of African villagers, and, of course, I particularly noticed his outlandish getup: the man was already wearing the bush hat that would become part of his legend, a threadbare velvet jacket, a striped undershirt whose consistently immaculate whiteness puzzled me throughout our successive encounters, along with an ordinary loincloth that he tied around his hips the way all the members of his generation do. He was like a caricature of the African peasant lost between two allegedly poorly reconciled or even possibly irreconcilable civilizations. I too (do I dare admit it?) unconsciously subscribed to this vision of the tragedy of African societies. In fact, the theme of acculturation, which had recently become fashionable in Saint-Germain-des-Prés and its surroundings, had already generated, among the enlightened partisans of dogma, a multitude of divergent, contradictory, intersecting, parallel, and complementary theses, whose proliferation left ordinary consumers of novelty like myself both dissatisfied and yet impregnated with their phantasmagoria.

In the day-to-day reality, besides being undermined by the inevitable nepotism of tyrannies, Africa was being bled dry by the massive draining of capital, gnawed away by the now practically institutionalized degeneracy of its corrupt elite, and devoured by the waste of its resources, all of which conspired to place the continent at the mercy of predatory foreigners. The combination of these cancers foreshadowed an inevitable metastasis and an ensuing coma. But no one seemed able to recognize these sad realities lived daily by the people. Were it not for the events recounted here, which amounted to a veritable revolution for the republic that finally inherited a press more audacious than free, the scholastic ramblings coming from abroad would have steadfastly continued their devastation. To have finally unveiled the African gangrene, too long hidden from the nations of the world, is not the least of the achievements of the men and women who will meet in this chronicle, these individuals who, at the start, were so unsophisticated, so timid, and so dispossessed, who created from scratch what the impenitent theorists, strangers on the continent but more peremptory than ever, would soon call, in their pompously vacuous language, the process of democratization.

At this point Zoaételeu had lived through only part of the adventures gathered in this account; all his brothers were dead; he was about seventy years old, had a dozen wives, maybe more, and some thirty children—excluding girls, of course, for they are not traditionally counted. He already had some sixty grandchildren, maybe more, almost all very young; and this time he was forced to count the girls as well, since, as he put it, they cost as much to send to school as the male children, and this modern age, cursed in more ways than one according to him, dictated that all children, irrespective of sex, had to be sent to school. He liked to say that things had really changed. He gave the impression of overdoing it a little to prime his image as the heroic and solitary champion of tradition. Nevertheless, he was all in all what he appeared to be, except when he was drunk.

It was a bout of inebriation, incidentally, that marked the beginning of his apotheosis—or his descent into hell, depending on one's point of view—if what I heard is true, that is. That event, which has since become legend in the province and maybe even in the republic, apparently happened in the following manner.

On the previous evening, Narcisse, one of the patriarch's sons, who, unlike his brothers, had chosen to live in town and who had, moreover, no particular profession, had arrived in the village to which his father had long been unsuccessfully trying to draw him. The patriarch's heart was always overjoyed whenever he was reunited with this cherished but rebellious son. He was loath to say it, however, or even to show it.

"For ages, I have been calling you to my bedside in vain," the patriarch told Narcisse, affecting the tremulous speech of the dying. "I guess you have finally agreed to come only because I have enticed you with the promise of money. No matter, you are here, and your poor mother and I are the happiest of parents because you can see us alive, probably for the last time. Who can foretell the hour when death will come knocking?"

It is beholden on all fathers, even those in the prime of life, to have these poignant talks with a prodigal child; there is nothing there to disturb the interlocutor, unless he has something on his conscience. Narcisse, who had something on his conscience, had attempted to shift the conversation as well as his gaze, which was of the swaggering and shifty type so typical of young urbanites.

"It is true that I have put aside some money for you," the patriarch continued, "but it is on condition that you use it in the way that I will tell you."

Narcisse had just had a conversation on this subject with his mother and his elder brother Zoaétoa, the most beloved of the children after Narcisse. Thanks to them, he already knew that he would reap nothing from this trip, and he was vexed.

"If you are trying to get me to mate with an ugly woman so that you can have more grandchildren, Father, that's crazy," he flared. "Where does anybody come off praising a woman just because she has wide hips that bode well for pregnancies? I know, you are going to tell me, as usual, that I should at least see her. You already know how I feel, and I have not changed my mind. There is more to life than children, Father. There are a thousand more important things. There is love, for one. If you don't mind, I'd first like to find a woman attractive before sleeping with her. That's very important, you know. A man is not some male dog . . ."

At this stage of the negotiations, the ritual required that the patriarch affect indignation. He complied.

"Is this any way for a son to speak to his father?" he exclaimed.

Seizing his opportunity, he embarked on a long tirade pep-

The Story of the Madman

pered with proverbs, anecdotes, and episodes from the ancestral epic. True to the tradition of an age-old rhetoric, he continued:

"Son, what makes you think you have more common sense than our predecessors? They were convinced there is nothing more noble or more useful to the community than producing children, than multiplying the number of men and women—especially men if possible. Multiplying the number of men is the most important thing in the world, more important than what you call love, my son. Yes, more than love. Because where there is a multitude of men, there is inevitably an abundance of generosity. Remember this well. They say that our ancestor, Zambo Menduga, a man who was taller than a baobab, the man from whom we all descend—you in the thirty-second generation, I in the thirty-first—was once surrounded by his enemies. The situation was critical and required the sacrifice of a warrior. Do you know, Son, how many of his children he had to ask before he found the one who would submit to the salutary act? Thirty-nine! Yes, Son, I said thirty-nine. If Zambo Menduga had only had fifteen children, or twenty-five, or thirty-five, our race would have been lost. Thank God, there were at least thirty-nine. And it was the thirty-ninth. . . ."

"But Father, those days are over. There are no more tribal wars, we are all citizens of one and the same republic now."

"There is no more war? So you think there is no more war, Son? Say it again that there is no more war. There is no more war, you say? Just listen to him. There is no more war, we are all citizens of one and the same republic. What next? There is no more war. . . . What about me then? Wasn't I imprisoned for six years? Since when can the head of a family, the most noble descendant of Zambo Menduga, be held six long years in an enclosure if there is no more war? There is no more war. . . ."

"No, Father, there is no more war. Even the resistance fighters, who were supposed to be invincible, have been crushed one after the other by the chief of state. It has been fifteen years since the last of their leaders was captured, condemned, and executed in the square of his native village. It's over, there is peace now; we must live in the present. And if there is another war one day, I will refuse to participate. I want to really live. I want love to be the real thing and not to copulate like an animal just to procreate. First of all, I don't like kids. That's my right, isn't it? I hate all kids. They're dirty, they shit, they squall. And they're expensive, Father, they have to be fed. Where do you want me to find the money? I live in the city. And just think, even water costs a fortune there. So, kids, you know . . ."

A unanimous, "Oh, oh, oh!" rose from the crowd of onlookers, always numerous whenever the prodigal son returned.

To save face, the patriarch would have had to raise the volume of his indignation a notch, to fly into a rage in fact. That would unfortunately have led to an inevitable falling out and, undoubtedly, to the abrupt departure of this too dearly loved but rebellious son, despite the late hour. Like most fathers, the patriarch did not wish to lose his stray sheep but rather to bring him back into the fold of rustic morality.

"Well, Son, go get some rest," the disillusioned father said, "but get up early tomorrow morning and come with me to the fields. We will savor some ancestral nectar there; it will improve your disposition, you'll see."

The ancestral nectar of the patriarch is known in everyday language as palm wine. The patriarch's usual breakfast consisted of a reckless intake of palm wine in the middle of nature and preferably at the break of day. Here was an ancestral rite Narcisse did not mind conforming to, anxious as he was to squeeze the juice from both city and village.

The following morning, on their return from the fields, a surprise awaited the patriarch and those of his children, including Narcisse and his older brother Zoaétoa, the son of his mother and the most beloved of the children after Narcisse, who, according to custom, had accompanied him there.

So as not to be alone in the middle of this family of peasants he did not cherish, Narcisse had brought along a young man cast in the same mold as himself, an urbanite with no definite profession, a crony to whose side lean times inexorably drew him back, and, moreover, someone as familiar as himself with shifty dealings and bent on challenging authority. This friend had slept late, as members of the breed tend to do. And while he was still in bed, a patrol of uniformed men parked its jeep by the side of the road and came to investigate the rumored presence in the village of individuals who did not ordinarily reside there. Accustomed to the permanent inquisition of the dictator's gorillas, the peasants customarily submitted without protest. They behaved accordingly.

Rudely awakened, the urbanite chose to take offense at the loutishness of the uniformed men and undertook to remind the representatives of the law of his rights. In response, the uniformed men pointed out to him, with long-winded eloquence, that they, on the other hand, enjoyed powers that had the peculiarity of brooking no argument. One thing leading to another, the altercation rapidly degenerated into a violent scuffle, undoubtedly to the satisfaction of the repulsive government gorillas, who were more than happy to practice their skills in the torture of rebellious crowds.

First the urbanite was roughed up in front of the villagers, assembled for the show. That soon lost its appeal.

All the males were ordered to line up as if for a parade; they were instructed to undress and to lie face down in the dust. Then the uniformed men set out to subject the women to the same treatment. A barely pubescent girl, who had resided in an establishment run by nuns and who was concealing her young breasts under the tatters of a filthy shirt, burst into tears and refused to comply. As one of the horrible government gorillas, probably the youngest of the lot but particularly excited, put his great paw on her shabby skirt, the barely pubescent adolescent pulled it down sharply over her legs and closed them tightly.

Instead of being moved by this behavior that was both charming and rarely encountered in our countryside, the ruffian, no doubt under the influence of early morning intoxication, slapped the barely pubescent adolescent repeatedly. At that precise moment, the patriarch, escorted by the troop of his children walking in a file and with whom he was gravely debating the virtues of ancestral morality, emerged from the woods. That, at least, was how the story was told to me.

The villagers claim that, had he been sober, things would have happened differently. The usually affable man would surely have been conciliatory toward the horrible government gorillas, as

The Story of the Madman

was in fact his habit. He would have invited them to his house; he would have offered them a few gourds of his famous ancestral nectar. And the whole thing would have ended joyfully amid hugs and renewed declarations of friendship. I do not believe it. Since the previous night, Zoaételeu had too insistently extolled those men of the past whose example he was urging his son to follow. Fate now challenged him to give a shining illustration of ancestral virtues; he was strutting in vain around this son who, thus far, had remained immune to his advances. He wanted finally to elicit his love and admiration, at any cost. He would have committed his folly sober.

However, the fact remains that he was not sober. He crossed the village square bellowing like thunder. He was no longer the old man with the irregular gait and the twisted carriage but the rowdy young man he had been for so long. With bulging eyes, flashing gaze, and lilting, springy steps, he stamped the native soil in the throes of a combative euphoria like the foaming torrent rushing from the mountaintop, roiling muddy waters that shatter all obstacles in their path.

"What is this I see?" the patriarch screamed. "What is this I see? Am I dreaming? Is everyone seeing what I am seeing? In this ancient domain, in my village, in my house, in front of me, right in front of me, they come to murder my children! Help, Zambo Menduga! Help, my valiant ancestors. . . ."

It seems hardly credible, when one recalls the period during which these events took place, a time when the terror inspired by the dictator had paralyzed the population. He marched right up to the uniformed man who had slapped his granddaughter and, without hesitation, slapped him repeatedly.

"I will teach you," he said as he struck him, "I will teach you, you who do not even know who your father is, I will teach you that this soil on which you have the great privilege of standing is the ancient domain of the noble lineage of Zambo Menduga. . . ."

The three uniformed men were at first practically paralyzed in astonishment, for their skill at brutalizing crowds was not as advanced as they had imagined.

When their reflexes finally kicked in, they all reached for

their belts at the same time, as they did during practice; they drew their guns out in unison and fired in the air, stupidly executing their drill by rote, and forgetting that their supply of ammunition was piddling and that their handguns were sparingly loaded, a fact that was not lost on the two urban louts. When these animals, realizing their mistake, attempted to retreat to the jeep, where they had left their more lethal weapons, determined now to save their skins valiantly by mowing down the crowd of unarmed peasants, as was their habit, the two city dwellers had beaten them to the arsenal and were carrying it away. The uniformed men tried to give chase; they were blocked by a wall of hostile villagers. They attempted to breach it by force. In the brawl that ensued and in which Zoaétoa, one of the patriarch's sons, distinguished himself and thus discovered his vocation for combat, the peasants and their hosts, deaf to all but the fighting instincts they had finally rediscovered, pummeled the uniformed men until the latter had absorbed the torrent of buried resentment magnified by twenty years of silence.

Then the villagers put the dictator–chief of state's men—unarmed, unrecognizable, with swollen faces and tattered uniforms, for once defenseless victims of the ferocity of the crowd—back in their jeep.

I was told that this is how the whole thing started. It is possible, now that I think about it.

Now they had to prepare for the reprisals of the uniformed men.

"All of you, take shelter in the forest, the traditional refuge of our ancestors," the patriarch ordered. "And I expect to be obeyed without question. As for me, I will remain here. I will be the thirty-ninth son of Zambo Menduga. I offer myself for the ultimate sacrifice since that is the price for the general salvation. Once they have drunk the blood of an old man, their sanity may return, and then, who knows, they may spare you. Now go, deep in the forest. . . ."

The village suddenly looked like a farmyard under attack by a bevy of predators. Mothers, one hand laden with bowls, the other dragging clusters of crying urchins, melted into the shadows of the foliage. Elderly villagers of both sexes, after a brief and spirited discussion, guardedly headed toward a mysterious destination. Young men, dressed as backup warriors, assembled in battalions before taking cover in the woods bordering the settlement, where they could keep an eye on their ancestor while keeping a lookout for the uniformed men.

They told me that, at first, the patriarch paced back and forth through the village, muttered curses, shook his fists, and defied the invisible government gorillas. Then he intoned a kind of chant in which I thought I recognized traces of an ancestral war chant resurrected from oral tradition. Soon, however, he squatted against a wall and appeared to doze off. Finally, when he awakened, he looked like a depressed old man, staring fixedly ahead as one aghast at the dawning awareness of reality.

However, nothing happened that day, to the astonishment of

18

the peasants but not to that of their city guests, who had been saying all along, "It's obvious that you do not know those animals. In all likelihood, they have not dared tell anyone about such a humiliating adventure, and they have gone into hiding until nightfall; or else, if they are smart, they have confided in a corrupt superior officer, who has said to them, 'I will take care of everything in exchange for a large chunk of your next paycheck.' In any case, this incident will have been kept from the great chief. That is the most likely scenario. They will, of course, get their revenge in the end, but they will do so through endless and underhanded harassment. Another hypothesis is that they have told the great chief everything, and he has said to them, 'You call yourselves soldiers? Where are your guns? You let some hicks strip you of your weapons and instead of fighting back you ran off like frightened gazelles. You heard me, frightened gazelles, that's what you are. You are not even worth the rope it would take to hang you!' And he has thrown them in the slammer. In that case, you will get what's coming to you, but as for us, we have accounts to settle back in the city with our own ruffians, who are of another breed, although not so different as all that. . . ."

In fact, in the dark hours of the following night, the two delinquents vanished like ghosts. Zoaétoa, the most beloved of the patriarch's sons after Narcisse, took a very harsh view of this defection, for he had just experienced the revelation of his vocation as a warrior.

"You can't abandon your people right before a battle," he confided to anyone who would listen. "You would not find me abandoning my family when it's time to fight. We are about to face the enemy, and what do they do? They take to their heels like frightened gazelles. Now I am a true warrior, and the fracas of an approaching elephant does not intimidate me."

His listeners, the patriarch included, were inclined to share this assessment and to feel a certain admiration for its author.

However, the aftermath of these events mostly bore out the deserters' prediction. The incident was, in fact, kept hidden from the great chiefs of the garrison, but they eventually caught wind of it, although not for several long weeks. They ordered an investigation that did not uncover the truth. But they remained distressed and troubled by the rumors. It was an affair of unprecedented gravity, highly damaging to the army's honor, if in fact it was true that elite troops had been disarmed, during a tussle, by ignorant peasants unfamiliar with the subtleties of the military arts.

They decided to come to the village to interrogate the peasants. Since they knew from professional experience that they would probably run up against a conspiracy of silence, they resolved to use the so-called strategy of gradual, oblique, and circuitous encirclement. That is how it came about that the great chief of the neighboring garrison made an entrance into the village that is forever engraved in the collective memory of the villagers. He was surrounded by his entire staff, preceded by two troop carriers crammed with soldiers, and followed at a distance by four light armored cars and three self-propelled rocket launchers. The soldiers, in combat uniform, sprang out from under the tarpaulins as if for action and quickly formed a corridor for the great chief and his entire staff to enter the village.

The great chief did not exactly fit the villagers' conception of a warrior figure, as they might envision him in their nightmares. He was of slight build, unimpressive height, had delicate features and a languid gaze, and although he spoke the language of the territory perfectly and fluently, he did not look like the native son he was.

Unlike his men, with their jutting necks, scowling faces, and prowling fox miens, the great chief advanced nonchalantly, not like a conqueror striding across the battlefield but rather like a young man eager to meet the little fiancée chosen for him by the areopagus of elders. But he was indeed the great chief, there was no doubt about that. He walked ahead of his men and was, moreover, the only one with five gold bars on his shoulders.

The officers had trouble hiding their skeptical admiration or, rather, their admiring skepticism as they watched the comings and goings of the rustic community that was rumored to have disarmed their men, reputedly some of the best-trained and most experienced soldiers around. As usual, the youngest children, followed by their school-aged siblings, who had been released by their teachers as soon as they had heard of the soldiers' arrival, soon crowded around the newcomers; then the men and women, responding to a signal that had gone unnoticed by all the officers except for the great chief, who was indeed a native of the area, came out of the woods one after the other and timidly approached the soldiers, convinced that the hour of retribution had caught up with the village but resigned to die with the patriarch, since that was their destiny.

The great chief boldly accosted Zoaételeu, the patriarch, and asked him a question, then another, then a third, then a fourth, then a fifth, then a sixth, all apparently innocuous, but actually loaded with implications and unsuspected traps, as he had been taught to do in military school. Zoaételeu's answers were all adequate, all courteous, and all spontaneous. The patriarch's boundless and elusive eloquence captivated the great chief and amused his men, without, however, erasing their sinister expressions.

But, without any shadow of a doubt, some sort of miracle was unfolding before the eyes of the tribe, gathered to hear the fatal verdict, as if the manes of the ancestors had enveloped the patriarch with an aroma made up of magical fumes. In response to an order shouted to no one in particular and in a language still unidentified to this day, the soldiers broke rank and promptly jumped over the slatted sides of the trucks to disappear under the tarpaulins. The great chief's staff returned to the vehicles they had arrived in, with the exception of the great chief's conveyance. The officers' cars, the troop carriers, the self-propelled rocket launchers, and the light armored cars turned around and drove off; the occupation of the rebel territory had barely started when it came to a halt. They say that a whole hour after his men and his entire staff had departed, the great chief was still conversing with the patriarch, next to whom he had sat down. Finally, they shook hands, but not without profusely congratulating each other. And that is how Zoaételeu and the military great chief, who should have led the reprisal strike warranted for an offense unprecedented even in the agitated history of the young republic, formed a friendship that

The Story of the Madman

was, at the very least, suspect, as it would appear to the quali-fied men later charged with the task of assessing it.

It is a fact that, following this incident, the colonel in charge of the neighboring garrison frequently visited Zoaételeu, sur-rounded at first by his command staff with their scowling faces and their prowling fox miens, then accompanied only by two men in civilian clothes, who may not even have been soldiers despite their remarkably broad shoulders, and finally alone and, amazingly, dressed in civilian clothes. Yet it has not been ade-quately noted that this evolution did not reassure the patriarch, even though the colonel never failed to bring a gratuity or a gift, most often consisting of bottles of whiskey or of some other liquor for which the patriarch had a well-known weakness. In return, Zoaételeu offered his ancestral nectar for the colonel's delectation. But, at each visit, the colonel would unfailingly bring up a subject that seemed to obsess him. For, true to his strategy of gradual, oblique, and circuitous encirclement, which the patriarch theoretically did not suspect, the officer would question Zoaételeu once the euphoria of inebriation had seem-ingly drawn them into a close intimacy:

"Are there any weapons in your village, o abyss of wisdom?"

"Weapons?" the patriarch would reply, feigning surprise and even indignation. "Oh, you mean the old shotguns we used in the past to protect our fields from monkeys. Incidentally, there are no more monkeys. I don't know how it happened, but they have suddenly disappeared from our forest. . . ."

"Tell me, old man, are there many hunting rifles in your vil-lage?" the obstinate colonel would continue.

"Don't talk to me about that, my son. It all started with the first troubles, twenty-five, maybe thirty years ago. At that time, Son, there was a great white military chief in charge of the gar-rison you now command. He came here, he called us together. He said to us, 'Give me your weapons. Bandits may come in the night to snatch them from you and use them to murder people. That is what they do everywhere. . . .' To tell you the truth, there was only one in the village, an old hunting rifle that enabled us to eat venison from time to time. It belonged to my brother Enoah. He was a great hunter, my brother, but he is dead. All my brothers are dead, my son. Yes, sir, what you see here is a lonely man. Can you only imagine how sad it is to be a lonely old man, without even one brother to console me?"

"And did he give up his rifle?"

"To the great white chief? Of course. How could he do otherwise? The white man had his name listed on his registers, since buying a rifle required authorization. So the names of rifle owners, as well as their villages, were documented. And it was easy to trace them. Great white chiefs were worse than the devil, my son. There was no way to escape his investigation, believe me. Ah, believe me, Son, my brother Enoah was a great hunter, but he died a long time ago. At least he did not have to go through what we have endured since."

"So there are no weapons here now?"

"No, my son, there are no weapons here now. There have not been any since then. Why do you ask, my son? Are the powers-that-be afraid of something?"

"No, on the contrary," the colonel confided one day. "On the contrary, everything is fine, and things will change for the better from now on. No one will come to harass you anymore, I guarantee it."

Whereupon the officer, alluding to a palace revolution that had recently taken place, informed the patriarch that grave events, which had gone completely unnoticed in the village and in the province, had occurred in the capital and had brought about upheavals in the upper echelons of the republic; they were the symptoms of an instability that would prove chronic. In his opinion, these events heralded the peaceful, harmonious, and secure future that had been denied the population for so long. The matter apparently held no interest for Zoaételeu: having erected as many concentric walls as generations around him, his descendants, led by Zoaétoa, his favorite son after Narcisse, had resolved to protect him from the delirious madness that city dwellers call politics. This poison was about to be injected into an innocent community by the daydreams of an officer of no substance.

"An old man like you, the wisest of the wise, must be in-

The Story of the Madman

formed every day of the major happenings in the nation. I must see to it."

He returned the following day with two young men carrying a television set and a car battery. For an hour, the colonel's companions made an earnest effort to initiate some of the adult sons of the patriarch—handpicked by him as being the most educated, on the pretext that they had gone to school longest —in the operation of these two apparently mysterious objects. However, they disappointed their instructors. The latter then undertook to test the villagers, who had all gathered around as usual and who were full of curiosity. It immediately became apparent to them that the youngest inhabitants of the village were the quickest to assimilate their teachings; although they had never been near a television set, they behaved as if they had been familiar with it for a long time.

To Zoaétoa's chagrin, for he harbored an instinctive dislike for the officer, the colonel gradually fell into the habit of lingering in the village, for the pleasure, as he put it, of watching the swarm of children, at their best behavior, seated each evening in the front row of viewers gathered in the patriarch's home. This spectacle had, for some time, inspired in the officer, who was a father himself, bold reflections concerning the younger generations and their future and gradually extending to the necessity of progress on the continent.

The colonel was nothing less than a man of principle. In truth, though he did not admit it to himself, he was weary of a military career for which no family tradition nor any philosophical consideration, derived either from education or spontaneous deduction, had prepared him and which, until now, had consisted largely of the deliberate perpetration of often bloody acts of brutality ordered against mostly destitute and innocent populations, the very people whom the forces of order should have made it their duty to protect and educate, in his opinion.

If he was optimistic about the recent political turn of events, it was because, like all true Bantus, the colonel was convinced that God placed us in this world mainly to enjoy its pleasures, and the patriarch's village was not parsimonious with them.

The Story of the Madman

"My son," Zoaételeu said to him one day, "do you know that you are not bad-looking? I'm sure that you have made more than one female heart in the village beat faster. Don't be shy on my account. If need be, honor me with your confidences; I will be your indulgent accomplice. I was young once myself, I know what it's like."

They say that the colonel accepted with alacrity, but for a long time it was not known whom he had chosen. It is, however, a fact that he suddenly fell into the habit of returning to the village incognito at night, sadly forgetting the precepts of military discipline and succumbing, almost without a fight, to the call of pleasure.

WHEN ZOAÉTELEU told the colonel that there were no weapons in the village, he was not being crafty, in this instance anyway. The two urban delinquents had taken away the arsenal acquired after the pitched battle against the uniformed men. It consisted of three ordnance pistols, three assault rifles, sixty grenades and a grenade launcher, three automatic pistols, a light machine gun, a rocket launcher, and a mortar, all in perfect condition and with enough fire power to storm a Bastille. The carnage that would have decimated the patriarch's tribe had these toys not been pinched by the two scoundrels does not bear thinking about. Knowing full well the general moral fiber in the dictator's army, since a number of their cohorts were in its ranks, the two urban delinquents had immediately begun to try to cash in their loot upon returning to the capital.

After endless caresses, including the surrender of their own bodies as one must do with city girls, they maneuvered the female relative of an old dipsomaniac sergeant, the self-proclaimed uncle of a young officer known for his excessive taste for philandering and himself an army buddy of a lieutenant who was well known in the inner sanctums of the ministries and was, moreover, the friend or relative of a noncommissioned officer believed to be the informant, albeit an accommodating one, of the minister of defense, if not of the president of the affected garrison, himself. That is the sort of people whose traces the two scoundrels habitually followed.

"Now, you understand? When you leave here, go directly to the old man's place," they advised the young woman in a tone of camaraderie mixed with menace. "Be sure not to let on where you got your information, all right? Just tell him, 'By chance, I met some guys who claimed they could persuade a friend of theirs, who knows close acquaintances of the fellows in possession of the stolen weapons, to return them to their owners. But they said that the friend told them that the fellows holding the weapons, who are not themselves the thieves of course, said that in order to return them, a small reward and a great deal of discretion would be welcome.'"

The investigation was concurrently running its course in the garrison. Masters at dissimulation and illicit solidarity, the soldiers had succeeded in fending off a weapons inventory for quite a while by means of endless evasive tactics. The talent of the troops in this republic to deceive and ridicule their superiors is mind-boggling. Nevertheless, the promptest retrieval possible of the sizable arsenal abandoned with the peasants would miraculously and definitively put the culprits out of trouble by providing an outright and incontrovertible denial to the rumors that were upsetting and irritating the high command.

It was an extremely comical situation, unparalleled perhaps in the universal annals of armies. The fate of these weapons had woven an infinite number of threads made up of maneuvers, intrigues, haggling, rivalries, and greed, implicating so many people and cronies among the riffraff and the public at large that, at a certain point, everyone within a hundred-kilometer radius, especially in the capital, knew what had happened.

The commotion was particularly acute among the lower-ranking officers of the police force, who are more prone to action than to thought. They plotted on street corners and in local bars, where they rehashed often extravagant rumors. The two delinquents' loot consisted of entire cases of weapons worth a fortune on the black market, where demand was high; they knew where the two rogues hung out; they were going to corner them and force them to share, and they might even discreetly make them cough up the goods. Young and not-so-young loafers, delinquents of all stripes, streetwalkers, schoolchildren, and high school pupils were openly jubilant, without, however, betraying the secret; they found in this affair a sort of revenge that an outsider, uninitiated in their unfathomable frustrations, could not possibly understand. One group knew the details of the clash in the village and made a melodrama of

The Story of the Madman

them; everyone was moved by the girl that a lout had pawed. Another group recalled, with hilarity and ever more realistic and spicy details, how a wave of enraged peasants had overwhelmed the frail patrol.

In the offices of the various ministries, in the banks, in the state enterprises, in the shops, among those whose profession calls for planning and cautious foresight, people gravely shook their heads over what was seen as a sign of a turning point in the destiny of the republic—bare-handed, simple men had raised the wall of their finally exhausted patience before the military, which had pitifully crashed into it.

While everyone knew that the weapons were right in the city, only the higher-ranking officers of the army, and especially those in command of the garrison concerned, were navigating in the fog.

This strange situation had the characteristics of a spreading earthquake, of the insidious infiltration of eroding waters, an imperceptible propagation of mephitic miasma, and of the throbbing thundering of a distant herd. That, at any rate, is how it was described by a young lawyer who would play a significant role in subsequent events; this incident, he added, announced an era that had been hopelessly awaited and would now be impatiently expected. It had taken no more than that to trigger the disintegration of a reign and Nero's downfall. First, he said, respectable folks had suddenly felt stifled, the armies had awakened from their protracted, indolent debauchery of old and had made the ground tremble with the barbaric march of the empire. Finally, the monuments and marble palaces had been shaken by an earthquake and immediately after laid to waste by a tidal wave.

"You take your wishes for reality," people said to the young lawyer.

"You'll see," he answered.

Events did not bear out his predictions right away. The delinquents' friend did not notify her uncle, the old dipsomaniac sergeant with whom she lived (things could never be that simple in this country); she immediately repaired to the home of her paramour, an ex-captain and a hero of the repressive campaigns against the western underground forces just before and after independence, who had since fallen into gangsterism. The two of them remained in seclusion the entire afternoon. The delinquents discreetly observed the dealings of the young woman and of the officer-gangster. At dusk, the officer-gangster went to see a buddy who had followed the same military and social path as himself. Having entrusted the surveillance of the prostitute to his associate, Narcisse shadowed the degenerate officer; disguised as a harmless passerby, he saw the two men in animated discussion on the brightly lit balcony of a modest villa. There was no doubt about it, they were planning a holdup.

Around midnight, the degenerate officer returned home with an enormous bearded character whom he had picked up, apparently by chance, at a dive, but who must have been an old accomplice always on the ready for nefarious doings and whom our delinquent recognized as a French mercenary exceedingly fond of little prepubescent African girls prodigally adept at acts of fellatio and notorious in the small world of white immigrants. Narcisse, following in their tracks, was then reunited with his friend, still lying in wait in the shadows, and learned from him that the girl had not set foot outside. The two delinquents waited for the enormous bearded character to leave the premises. Then they barged into the detached pavilion where the officer apparently lived alone, but which was not, in all probability, his residence, and beat him to a pulp.

"Don't even dream of betraying us again," they told their not-so-faithful friend in a tone that chilled her blood like a death sentence.

She resigned herself to sharing her secret with her uncle, the old dipsomaniac sergeant, probably the only simple man in this universe, who contacted his cousin, the young lieutenant fond of philandering adventures. The latter decided that this was his big chance: he would confiscate the loot and pocket the spoils. He informed the old dipsomaniac sergeant that he would not lift a finger unless he met the interested parties, as he called them.

"Out of the question!" Narcisse responded. "A colonel, maybe, someone with access to discretionary funds, all right. But a little penniless lieutenant, no way. What I want is some-

The Story of the Madman

one who's rolling in dough. A man with dough, dammit! Not a deadbeat."

For weeks, the young lieutenant fond of philandering adventures gave no sign of life.

"It's a fit of spite," the old dipsomaniac sergeant said. "Put yourselves in his place. I'm working him over; he'll come around, you'll see."

The young lieutenant finally agreed to take the offer to his comrade at the ministry, in return for the promise of a fat commission.

"Your timing is perfect," his comrade, the lieutenant at the ministry, said. "In fact, you're a godsend. A client has been pestering me for months."

The client was a rich Syrian businessman, who had given asylum, in violation of immigration laws but with the protection of the titular minister of the Department of the Interior, to seven dissident Hezbollah fighters, who are, as everyone knows, rapacious consumers of instruments of death. From that point on, the negotiations went smoothly, for the Syrian businessman did not hesitate to commit himself to the old dipsomaniac sergeant, whom he visited in the latter's shanty and whose daughters he was not loath to fondle.

A deal was finally struck, to the relief of our two delinquents, whose cash reserves were suddenly and providentially supplemented, although not to the point of filling their coffers. So many people had been involved in the transactions that, after everyone had been remunerated, Narcisse was left with very little profit.

Moreover, this last feat was accomplished during a very difficult period. An economic and financial crisis had overtaken the republic. Everyone was left to face it in whatever way possible, and the delinquents' traditional sources of revenue were drying up one after the other. The regular trade of elegant rogues like Narcisse foundered into a slump like all the other activities.

What Narcisse and others like him called love is surely not qualified as such in most languages spoken by human beings. As long as he dressed in the latest fashion, any relatively well-read young man, who often had a secondary school diploma or was even sometimes more or less regularly enrolled at the National University, could easily enter into a liaison with the wife, the live-in partner, or simply the favorite mistress of a powerful and rich man who was almost always someone close to the center of power.

Taking advantage of the African tradition whereby kinship constitutes an inescapable web even for Africans themselves, the young woman would introduce her lover to her powerful protector as her brother or as some other close relative. The elegant and educated young man would then attach himself to the powerful man and display a boundless devotion to him. He would follow in his footsteps everywhere. He would make himself indispensable by doing him various small favors such as assuming the duties of chauffeur or those of various other servants when they were on vacation, while ensuring with very subtle skill that no one could confuse him with a servant at social events or at official gatherings. In order to accomplish this, he needed only to sit next to the powerful man, either in the adjacent armchair or on the same sofa, to request the same drinks as the powerful man from the hostess or the master of ceremony, and not to wait to be invited to take a seat once dinner was served but rather to sit down at the table at the same time as the most select guests. He would take the choicest cuts; he was a relative of the guest, so no one dreamed of protesting, not even the protector, who, though surprised, was powerless in the face of tradition.

Sometimes the guileless protector would remunerate the young man of indefinite status for his services. Usually the latter shared the liberality of the powerful man with his female accomplice. Once he had become the intimate and confidential friend of the rich man, the elegant delinquent of indefinite status would lie in wait with the rapacity of the tiger tempered by the patience of the boa for the opportunity to wheedle a large sum of money from his beautiful friend's protector. He would then disappear, only to resurface in another city of the republic or, more often, in another more or less distant African republic as the owner of a taxi or of some other similar enterprise.

The Story of the Madman

The excessively timorous Narcisse, who was more at ease behind the scenes, where he was a virtuoso, and who was instinctively shy of the footlights, had never dared take the plunge. He had successively been the paramour of several women, each change propelling him into ever higher social and political circles.

Jeanne, his partner of the moment, was suddenly abandoned by her protector, a major director of a bankrupt state enterprise forced to shut down. So Narcisse found himself, in effect, unemployed. Ignorant of the cruel laws of the free market, the young man never questioned his ability to quickly overcome his misfortune. And as often happens in such cases, he at first strove only nonchalantly and confidently, then more and more desperately and frantically, to find a taker for the only thing in this world he had to sell, as the financial climate continued to deteriorate.

Finally, unable to scrounge up even one meal a day, three months overdue in his rent, and at the end of his rope, Narcisse agreed to become the assistant of his inseparable crony, who was now a service station attendant. After one short month, he decided that it was more than he could take. That was when he suddenly experienced what might be called his epiphany.

"We are going to the country," he told Jeanne one morning, out of the blue.

"What country?" demanded the young woman, who was born in the city and had never lived anywhere else.

"Just do as you're told," Narcisse replied in the authoritative tone common among his type. "We're going to the country, period!"

And so it was that several months, perhaps even a year, after the events related at the beginning of this chronicle, the patriarch saw his son Narcisse alight from a car accompanied by a young woman whom the villagers, briefed by the educated members of the tribe, soon named "the Parisian," because she was such a fashion plate with her leather miniskirt, her red sweater stretched taut over an aggressively bountiful bosom, and her shiny ankle boots.

No DOUBT about it, this must be one of those women who inspire love, that new breed his son Narcisse had invented—taut breasts under chic, form-fitting clothing that showcased an abundant bosom and invited the caressing hand, round smooth legs jutting from under a very short skirt that made them seem to go on forever, and a girlish, prancing gait that age would never change. It was like a dreamworld the patriarch could only explore with his eyes half closed, his lips quivering in an evanescent smile. He marveled, though without getting carried away, as if vapors from his forgotten youth at moments fused with Jeanne's image. A woman who inspires love is a woman one would not share with anyone for anything in the world, not even with a brother. One walks side by side and hand in hand with her, as he had often seen Narcisse and Jeanne do in front of him, and one embraces her suddenly, just like that, as if stung into it, without worrying about being laughed at by everyone around.

"If I were my son, I wouldn't want to share her with anyone either," the patriarch ruminated.

Having made this leap into unfamiliar territory, Zoaételeu was convinced he had crossed over half, if not the entire, distance separating him from his beloved yet distant son. However, subsequent events would plunge him into an increasingly dark abyss of confusion.

Far from displaying his usual impatience to leave, Narcisse seemed inclined to prolong his stay and even to settle down, but in a way that scandalized the family, although no one ever openly discussed it. So as to be accepted by the community,

Jeanne had quickly learned the ways and customs of the place. However, she, alone among the women, dared to criticize her man bluntly. The conflict between them remained latent until, one day, it erupted in a particularly virulent scene that awakened Zoaételeu's prudence.

"Hey listen, don't you think you should quit sitting there all day next to your old man?" the young woman, half joking, half exasperated, said to her man. "You're not old! You need to get going, finally. There's work to do, as if you didn't know. Look at all the others."

"Bravo, you hick," Narcisse replied with a sneer. "Bravo! So you're turning into a real backwoods woman. You wear the back basket, you wield a hoe, you start fires in the dirt like a real savage. That's good, that's very good. Manual labor, my girl, there's nothing like it. At least, that's what they teach in school. But in the meantime, will you leave my father and me the hell alone? With your birdbrain, how could you possibly expect to understand why we sit here together all day long? Well, I'll tell you, we are settling the details of my inheritance. Can you understand that?"

"Inheritance? You must take me for a complete idiot. What is there to inherit here? The baobabs? The catfish in the rivers? The snake-infested bush? Talk about gold mines! And all you have to do is to reach down. So how come you don't even reach down then? You have no dignity."

"He is not completely wrong for once," the patriarch intervened good-naturedly. "So you think that there is nothing to inherit here, my girl. Well, it does seem that way, you're right. But, just think, behind every bush, behind every baobab, there is a ghost watching us, the ghost of an ancestor. You can't see them, all those ghosts, but they can see you. Isn't that an inheritance?"

"Really?" the young woman answered, both deferential and skeptical. "What you say is probably true, Papa, but still, you're encouraging him to be lazy. That's not right. Your son is lazy. He has to be nagged all the time."

The ancestors' ghosts were not the only invisible things in the village. A number of other phenomena, unrelated to the after-world, had escaped the notice of the young city girl, whose innocence usually charmed the patriarch and confirmed Narcisse's disdain for the weaker sex.

"It seems as if . . . ," the patriarch began to say, after Jeanne had walked away.

"As if she suspects something, Father? No way. Those animals are not like your women here. You wouldn't believe how aggressive ours are. Even if she did suspect something, if some scatterbrain blabbed something to her, or if she spied an unusual posture, a furtive entrance or exit, or I don't know what else, do you think that she would be angry enough to assault me? Absolutely not. We know each other inside out, you know. There is a pact between us. Don't you worry about it."

A scheme united the finally reconciled father and son, since a peace treaty had promptly followed Narcisse's capitulation, which he had indicated immediately upon his return to the fold. In a spirit of self-denial Zambo Menduga himself must have applauded in the underworld, Narcisse had immediately settled down to the task of fulfilling the principal clause.

She was a very young adolescent but tall, and trained to face all of life's events with resigned courage. She was even uglier than Narcisse had imagined and looked like a cross between a giraffe, with her endless neck and her narrow face imperfectly plastered on a minuscule skull, and a prehistoric female gorilla, with her huge rump and her thick legs planted on feet the size of tennis rackets. As a precaution, the patriarch shrouded the girl's arrival in elaborate secrecy. He ordered that she remain secluded, and the two young people met alone during the day as soon as the villagers had gone into the woods. Although Narcisse had been an assistant gas-station attendant only long enough to grow disgusted with the nightmarish job, it had nevertheless toughened him up to face other frightful missions, as long as they were lucrative. And this one was, thank God.

Who can imagine the extremes to which elegant but impoverished young scholars in African cities were reduced when crisis gripped the continent in the late eighties of this calamitous century?

This series of heroic sacrifices gradually placed Narcisse into

The Story of the Madman

such an exalted state that upon his first meeting with the colonel, he thought of himself as a fearless man. It is true that the colonel was in civilian clothes and displayed none of his military attributes.

"You were missed, my son," the patriarch told the officer. "I have not stopped talking about you to my son here, who lives in town where he is studying. Every day I said to him, 'Today, for sure, my good friend, the great chief, will visit.' And every day we were very disappointed when you did not appear. What happened, my son? Have you been ill?"

"Not at all, venerable one. I simply had more work than usual, that's all."

Then, turning to Narcisse, the officer said in French, "So, you attend the university?"

"That's right," Narcisse replied. "Unfortunately, it's point-less these days. All the jobs are already taken. *Tarde venientibus ossa.** In the sixties or even the seventies, it was worthwhile enrolling in a military school for example. I would be a general today. Well, let's say a colonel, a colonel is not so bad either. They make a nice round salary. How much, by the way, Colonel? Seven, eight hundred thousand?"

"You exaggerate, young man," the colonel said with a cour-teous but cold smile.

"Yes, but there are fringe benefits also; free servants, lodg-ings likewise, service limousines. Four of them for a colonel, if I'm not mistaken. And most important, there is the privilege of discretionary funds. You can have as much funding as you want when you are a high-ranking officer, isn't that right, Colonel? Some people even say that these are nonrecallable loans, is that true? And let's not forget the fat commissions on arms pur-chases. I wouldn't mind being a colonel too and having as much dough as I want. My little Jeanne and I would have it made."

"You are already married?" the colonel asked as he unpacked some whiskey bottles.

*It would be erroneous to conclude from this quote—as I myself did initially—that it is indicative of a young man steeped in the humanities. It is listed in the pink pages of the standard Larousse dictionary along with its translation.—*Author's note*. Those who come late to the table get only the bones. —*Translator's note*

"Married, Colonel? What an idea! No, Jeanne is just a little sister, on my maternal uncles' side, you see. It's just that we have done all our studies together, even as kids. We are never apart; well, from time to time, but not often. Come to think of it, she should be here with us. Where did she go? Someone go find her!"

Jeanne docilely hastened to join them—she too ready, undoubtedly, for any eventuality. They gave her a drink just like the men who made up the usual company.

The colonel was in the throes of a secret torment. He took frequent small sips from his drink, and rather than settle back arrogantly in the wicker armchair that had, in effect, been his since the first day, he perched himself at its edge, stared straight ahead, laughed bitterly when he did laugh, and though he spoke little, he was inclined to a laconic intimacy as if he were looking for an exceptionally friendly ear, or a shared complicity.

"My son is racked by sorrows," the patriarch finally said to him, "but he does not want to admit it or to share his burden with his friends. Does the great chief doubt an old man's wisdom? Does he not know that his undeviating generosity has made me his ever devoted servant?"

"Actually, I have to leave you right away. That is what saddens me. Pressing and, believe me, very unfortunate engagements call me elsewhere without delay."

Speaking in French, Narcisse, whose head was easily affected by alcohol, said, "Come on, Colonel, you have said too much or too little. What is going on? When I left the capital a week ago, there were rumors everywhere of a putsch."

"Where did you get such nonsense, boy!" the colonel replied, also in French, apparently annoyed by the young libertine's effrontery.

The officer got up, to answer a natural physical need he said, and went out. As soon as he was outside he felt the caress of the cool night air. It seemed to him that he was experiencing a happiness one could only encounter once in a lifetime. The moon was out; the rhythms of a traditional dance accompanied by children's or women's voices, and sometimes by both, animated the village with a crystalline innocence, drowned every now and then by the passing roar of a car engine. The colonel approached the group of dancers and proceeded to distribute banknotes, as was the custom with high-ranking dignitaries, to the deafening cheer of the recipients.

After stretching under the moonlight and doing some limbering exercises, which the peasants took for propitiatory rites, the colonel docilely returned to his seat between the patriarch and Narcisse. As usual, Zoaételeu's perennial guests were noisily conversing, divided into groups that successively ignored, insulted, or mutually applauded each other over points of ideology. The colonel leaned over to speak in the patriarch's ear, inviting Narcisse with a look to share in the confidence.

"I have an old and close friend who is perhaps about to make a big mistake."

"An officer?" Narcisse asked.

The colonel nodded.

"I see what's going on, Colonel!" said Narcisse, now in the grip of incipient intoxication and speaking French again. "I see what's going on. Well, I'll tell you something. Distance yourself from that individual immediately. He's going to make a fool of himself, a real fool! I tell you, someone in your position should never take risks, you know what I mean? This will get you nowhere, or it will land you in a real mess you won't soon get out of. Think of all those poor devils you have been helping and who wait for you every day like some messiah—my old father here, myself, my little sis Jeanne. . . . And what would become of them if you took a fall? What would become of them? What would become of us? Did you ever think about that?"

The patriarch was as intrigued by the poignancy of the gestures and facial expressions as by the enigmatic sounds of a language to which he had never had any access. Words, images, and convoluted twists had to be invented to make him understand the colonel's torment.

The patriarch lapsed into a long meditation in a silence respected by the colonel, Narcisse, and effortlessly by Jeanne, who was more faithful than ever to her deplorable status. Finally, the patriarch uttered his oracular words:

"Nothing is true and nothing is certain except the lessons transmitted by the ancestors: they must be heeded in all circumstances. People say that when Zambo Menduga was uncertain, he would go to sleep to await the visit of the great ancestors. They would appear to him in a dream and dictate the right course to him. Why didn't the great chief's bosom friend do this? Why did he not go to sleep and await the visit of the ancestors? Does he even have any?"

The colonel was speechless.

"No, no, no," Narcisse intervened in French. "Stay away from that troublemaker, I tell you. Stay with us tonight. Jeanne will keep you company if necessary. Don't let yourself get pulled into the shit. . . ."

The colonel only partially acquiesced to Narcisse's strategy, however. He decided to leave. His men had been patiently waiting for him in a limousine parked by the side of the road. As he approached, one of them opened a door with that casual deference of protocol. But the colonel suddenly changed his mind, turned back, and asked Jeanne to come keep him company. With alacrity, Jeanne hurriedly gathered a few things and, to the astonishment of the villagers, who had witnessed the various stages of this scene thanks to the moonlight, disappeared into the service limousine. The purring of the motor faded slowly in the night.

I CANNOT BEGIN to say how curious I was to find out what everyone had felt and how they had reacted after this incident. I imagined that the villagers were thrown into a protracted state of shock by this brutal revelation of urban morals. And had the patriarch not been obliged to summon his son sharply and demand to be told how one could, at the same time, love a woman and share her?

I even imagined what the delinquent's retort would have been.

"Listen, Father, I did say that love had to be reckoned with, because a man is not an animal or he wouldn't be a man, but I never said that Jeanne and I are in love. Walking hand in hand with a woman, even falling in her arms a hundred times a day, doesn't mean you love her."

Or else, he could have answered in a style consistent with the outrageous picture I had of him:

"Father, you are not going to tell me that the sharing of women is news to you. I know very well that it has always been done here. Any number of Zambo Menduga's supposed descendants were born that way. You have often told us so yourself, don't you remember? I'm not surprised! With you, booze and memory don't make a good pair. And why did our great ancestor do that? For the same reason I do, Father, for the dough or something like it. Money is the name of the game, old man!"

It must be noted, in fact, that the community knew nothing about the extent of the scandal, and no arguments, not so much as an oblique remark, pitted the patriarch against Narcisse.

They took in those events, it seems, just as they happened. No one took the trouble to set them side by side or to compare them one to the other, like so many bits of furniture, for fear of assembling a monster instead of the boy they had always known and whom everyone wanted to continue to cherish forever. As if by tacit agreement, Narcisse's character did not come into sharper focus with Jeanne's departure, nor did it appear plainly for what it was, but remained as vague as ever to his kinsmen.

The whole affair was soon consigned to oblivion by the swirling vicissitudes of daily life. Since her rival had, to all intents and purposes, forfeited the game, the little fiancée imposed by Zoaételeu was now able to come out in the open and was joyfully welcomed by the villagers; this simple, ugly girl was as reassuring as a deformed but familiar plant. Without going so far as to disavow her, Narcisse avoided as much as possible compromising himself at her side, while on her part, she deployed treasures of imagination and feminine guile in order to project the image of a couple with this man on whom she had so long and so imprudently focused her dreams.

It was cacao season, and although there had never been very much in the village, the whole province was infused with a festive excitement that made everyone forget for two months the tedium and deprivation of the remainder of the year.

The attraction of the long feast, which even before the recession had drawn young urbanites from the province back to the fold, swelled the neighboring clans with noisy hordes of prodigal children of the same breed as Narcisse. The peasants observed with dread this restless, motley band in whom they were unable to recognize themselves but who continued unaccountably to arouse their pride. These guests did not speak a language accessible to common mortals, had no set time for sleeping, no religion, no great urge to work, no discipline in their lives, no fear of offending, and yet everyone loved them. Narcisse jumped at the chance of joining his old cronies and returning to old habits of aimless roaming and drunken sprees.

In fact, he disappeared suddenly. Everyone thought that he

The Story of the Madman

had finally grown tired of his imposed fiancée and had gone back to Jeanne. Even when news of the putsch and its miraculous consequences reached them, Narcisse's whereabouts remained unknown. That may even have been what saved him.

He was not at the side of the patriarch or of the colonel when the latter, a newly appointed minister, came with a noisy escort, presided over by Jeanne in the role of grande dame, to render homage to the old friend who had given him such judicious advice. How many presents rained daily on the patriarch's once impoverished, once denuded home! How many dignitaries honored his modest abode, which he steadfastly refused to abandon for the city villa in which the minister wanted to have him settle! The colonel and the patriarch were seen arm in arm on television, as well as in newspaper photographs.

The first concession Narcisse extracted from Jeanne, who obtained it effortlessly from her powerful protector, was to spend a few weeks in the former colonial state to paint the town red as he had always secretly dreamed of doing. However, behind-the-scene wheeling and dealing was his true vocation. When he returned to the republic, the colonel, who had recently been appointed minister of foreign affairs, was on an extended trip to the United States, where he had the difficult task of convincing a skeptical audience of the legitimacy of the new regime. Jeanne was his constant companion but managed to find time to lavish on the handsome Narcisse all the assurances of her passion, not to mention the guarantee of the highest protection the state could provide.

Narcisse could have lorded it everywhere, but, as a true son of Zoaételeu, the wisest of the wise, he was content to have it all, but always behind the scenes. From that position, he saw all the more clearly the depravity of the new leaders, which was in fact of the same nature as that which they had denounced in their predecessors.

The speeches, the television, the radio, and the newspapers, all under government control at that time, were filled with talk of austerity, of morality, of liberation, of revolution.

In fact, just like their predecessors, the new leaders looted the banks and the public funds and exported this money that could have been so useful to the country; for their personal enjoyment and away from prying eyes, they siphoned off billions of dollars from the oil revenue meant for the republic's coffers at the very moment they were steering the nation into the vortex of foreign debt; they built sumptuous homes for themselves and their families; they laid claim on the wives, the live-in partners, the girlfriends, and the mistresses of their opponents, and if the latter balked they landed on the dank pallets of sinister dungeons; it was the same for government jobs, as well as positions in large companies, which were distributed among relatives; they levied commissions on contracts with foreign corporations, making no exception for charitable organizations.

Rumor had it that the minister of public works tried to subject to that treatment—known euphemistically in Anglo-Saxon realms as a *racket*—a company commissioned by the Canadian government to modernize for free the capital's water supply system, a commodity that had been traditionally available only in unpredictable spurts. The virtuous company was scandalized and abandoned the project. The minister of public works instituted proceedings against the company on the grounds that it had unilaterally broken a contract. The Canadian government went out of its way, no one knew why, to spare the new administration, and the affair did not appear in the newspapers or cause a scandal, but it was for a long time the cause of much laughter among insiders until they just as mysteriously lost interest. The incident was soon forgotten, but, in Narcisse's opinion, the new government team was doomed to a short term. After all, did it not, like its predecessor, hold sensual frenzy, nepotism, and arbitrariness as its hallmarks? Until the next coup, he intended to reap the most out of the present state of affairs without compromising himself.

Moreover, it was rumored that officers and ministers who had survived the April putsch had been given asylum by a foreign power that was supplying them with weapons and money. Soon, the regime was forced into the humiliating position of having to expose its vulnerability by telling the public about a so-called neocolonialist conspiracy. This affair became the

The Story of the Madman

obsessive theme of passionate proclamations and entreaties accompanied by appeals to the patriotism of the populace. Narcisse was not deceived by the public's attitude. Mostly, the general mood seemed to be one of scornful indifference, but secretly the people hoped to see the new government receive a good lesson because it had deceived them with its demagoguery, although they harbored no illusions, meanwhile, about its opponents.

The suburbs, outlying districts, and slums lived in anticipation, with the result that lower-level government employees who lived there stopped going to their offices in the downtown area, or if they went, displayed an insurmountable apathy.

Toward the end, the mistresses of dignitaries began to leave in increasing numbers as did newly wealthy merchants and businessmen. Encouraged by the minister of foreign affairs, who had recently returned from a tour overseas during which he had been consistently snubbed, Jeanne left. Not bothering to wait for anyone's permission, Narcisse left on the same plane.

Since he had never gone back to see his father, the young man was not aware of the role the patriarch might be accused of playing in a regime in which the colonel held such a high rank. It did not even cross his mind to warn his father. Egotistical as he was, nothing short of a miracle could have induced him to worry about anyone but himself, and, on occasion perhaps, Jeanne.

Far from taking the capital by surprise, operation revenge came as a relief, like the downpour that heralds the end of a storm. The bulk of the enemy forces, which had entered from the south and made their initial advance under cover of the woods before coming out in the open on the roads, encountered no resistance. Upon meeting with the aggressors, government troops disbanded rather than fight, or else they deserted their units as they got closer to the front. The populations in the rural areas were unaware of these events, since they were not mentioned anywhere, owing to the draconian censorship imposed by the government on the press. In the capital, where the grapevine is usually the surest source of information, everyone knew exactly what was happening.

The Story of the Madman

Never before had our people been confronted with such a singular set of events. How could one fail to marvel at how well they maintained their composure under these unprecedented circumstances?

Since the television set in the village was no longer subject to the whims of the car battery now that a generator had been installed at the colonel's orders, Zoaételeu and his family lived hour by hour, like a calvary, the battle that toppled the new government.

During the evening news, which now routinely drew the entire tribe to the television, a richly bedecked character, resembling the colonel the first time he came to the village, was seen unfolding a sheet of paper and sternly reading a long proclamation. This was undoubtedly a dramatic event. The patriarch consulted his educated sector. Opinions were split. According to some, war had just been declared against a foreign nation; others claimed that, if there was in fact a war, it must be between the friends of the colonel and their enemies who had been ousted previously and who were now taking their revenge.

Although the screen went blank immediately after this, the entire tribe instinctively remained in front of the set without needing to discuss their course of action. Then the screen lit up again with images that horrified the innocent assembly. Columns of tanks and troop carriers with dark green tarpaulins raced down the streets. Helmeted soldiers ran, ducking behind walls every now and then; they quickly scaled obstacles; they set their machine guns and mortars into position and opened fire, their hands vibrating on the gleaming steel.

A raging fire engulfed the floors of an imposing building. Panicked civilians fled beneath swirling spirals of smoke, shielding their heads with their hands. Airplanes and machines that the patriarch's educated sector could not name—they were in fact helicopters—took turns streaking across the sky, every so often dropping objects that, upon striking buildings or homes, produced horrible explosions followed by billowing red flames, all of which were drowned out by the military music playing in the background; squares and sidewalks were littered with dislocated corpses. Pinned to the ground, a child opened a grimacing mouth, probably to let out a howl of pain and despair, one hand clenched on a leg where dark blood foamed from a gaping wound, the other hand stretched out toward the knight who was supposed to protect widows and orphans.

"This cannot be happening in our country, it is not possible!" a woman exclaimed, bursting into tears.

"It is too!" the ten educated villagers replied in unison. "We recognize the capital."

A cluster of decorated military men standing in front of a map conferred with each other, shaking their heads convulsively. An official in a suit and tie raised his arms to the sky in what was surely a sign of victory.

The screen went dark again and, after a long wait, lit up once more; the richly bedecked character reappeared; he was smiling. He made some statements that the educated villagers did not all understand in the same way, but the images that followed left little doubt that the colonel and his friends had been routed. The newly vanquished government was displayed to the viewers: in the center of the group stood the colonel, dressed in civilian clothes, disheveled, barefoot, head bowed, and unshaven. A helmeted soldier walked up to him and struck him on the temple with the butt of his gun. A grimace clenched the colonel's face, and he collapsed.

Then the screen showed a column of soldiers in fatigues, bareheaded, unshaven and barefoot, heads bowed, and as unkempt as the colonel. On an order issued by a drill officer, they squatted with their hands crossed over their heads; then, in one motion, they lay face down on the asphalt.

For a whole week, the screen was filled with more such images. Then life seemed to return to normal. All kinds of vehicles passed on the road. The villagers scattered into the woods at dawn. The patriarchs remained seated at their doorsteps all day. Patrols of uniformed men would arrive unpredictably, park their jeep by the side of the road, and proceed to search the houses while controlling the villagers. This harassment was the only language they knew, and apparently nothing would make them desist.

Now pregnant, the little fiancée inquired of every passing

traveler for news of her man. In the evening, the tribe gathered in front of the television set to watch the news, which, just as before, dealt almost exclusively with the subject of the chief of state, who was no longer the same one of course. To all appearances, life was back to normal, but appearances can be deceiving.

THE PERENNIAL PATROL of uniformed men, heading in a southerly direction, drove slowly by on the road before turning around and, still slowly, heading north; they stopped and parked their jeep by the side of the road. The usual three men making up a patrol jumped out of their vehicle, crossed the road, then the square, and approached the patriarch, who was seated at his doorstep, meditating.

"Would you please state your identity?" they said to the old man.

As he appeared not to understand, they asked, "What is your name?"

"What is my name?" the patriarch repeated, breaking into polite laughter. "You ask me what my name is, young men? No one has ever asked me that question before, not even when the white man was still ordering the black man around. And you, of all people, ask me a question that dishonors me?"

"Show us your identification card!" the uniformed men asked, unmoved by the patriarch's indignation.

"I don't know what you are talking about."

"What is your name?" the horrible thugs asked again in unison.

"You ask me my name, my children? Everyone within fifty kilometers knows my name. But, to my dishonor, you had to come here and address me like a bastard, with my children standing here to witness my decadence."

"Will you please state your identity?" the tenacious uniformed men persisted.

The patriarch's entourage was first to falter.

48

The Story of the Madman

"Father," said his granddaughter, who had once been slapped by an overzealous thug, "Father, tell them your name and let's be done with it," the frail child begged, backed by the chorus of the patriarch's many descendants, who had gathered in a circle around the old man.

Zoaételeu not only gave his name, he recited the lineage of his ancestors back to Zambo Menduga, learnedly enumerating the thirty generations that separated him from the divine forebear.

"Are you satisfied now?" he asked finally. "And if so, what do you want with me?"

"Our orders were just to gather this information for the records," they answered calmly. "As for the rest, expect a visit from the chief of the garrison, who will tell you what your fate will be."

Whereupon they took their leave, but courteously.

Two days later, the great chief of the neighboring garrison did indeed come to the village. He was surrounded by his entire staff, preceded by two troop carriers crammed with soldiers, and followed at a distance by four light armored cars and three self-propelled rocket launchers. The soldiers, in combat uniform, sprang out from under the tarpaulins as if for action and quickly formed a corridor for the great chief and his entire staff to enter the village.

The great chief did in fact exactly fit the image of a warrior, as the villagers might envision him in their nightmares: gigantic and beefy, his face crisscrossed with scars, the likes of which had not been seen for a long time among the noble descendants of Zambo Menduga, this officer, who did not speak a single word of the local language and whose statements were transmitted to them by an interpreter, did not appear to be, and in truth was not, a native son.

Cut from the same cloth as his entourage, with their jutting necks, scowling faces, and prowling fox miens, the chief advanced proudly, surveying his surroundings with an eagle eye, a true conqueror on the field of battle. He walked at the head of his escort and was the only one wearing the insignia of supreme

The Story of the Madman

command, five gold bars on each shoulder. He stopped in front of Zoaételeu, who was seated at his doorstep deep in thought; the officer gave the patriarch a long, cold look. Without speaking to him, he entered the sacred abode, like a tank bursting into a bunker.

The officers meticulously examined all the rooms of the modest home as well as all the outlying buildings and lingered around the generator and the television set. Then they formed a circle around the patriarch. They stared fixedly at the old man who was said to have inspired the actions of those the government-controlled media once called the blazing warriors of the revolution but who were now dubbed dirty criminals driven by ambition. For a brief moment, it appeared as if their persistent silence was inspired by a reverential awe. In reality, it was simply the subterranean boiling that foreshadows the explosive eruption of revenge, as the villagers would later explain.

The great chief handed down his verdict, which was translated thus by a haggard and stuttering interpreter:

"Old fetishist, your advice led once valorous officers into the madness of crime and tyranny. In return, you received the undeserved riches that fill your home as symbols of your unworthiness. The people have decided first of all to take back all these riches in order to teach posterity that the reward for abuse of power is gold cursed by God and man. You will subsequently be tried by a severe but just tribunal, which will undoubtedly condemn you to death."

They asked him, "Do you have anything to say?"

Nothing had ever prepared Zoaételeu for this situation, and the lore of tradition, even shored by the recollection of ancestral feats, was of little help. He lost himself in emphatic apothegms glorifying resignation to destiny and the happiness of dying with honor.

The patriarch's boundless and slippery eloquence did not captivate the great military chief, nor did it amuse his men, who saw it as the defiance of an old man imbued with magical powers and who, consequently, deserved an exemplary punishment.

On an order from the great chief, they took each and every

object that could testify to the privileged status the patriarch had enjoyed during the period when the colonel honored him with his friendship and his protection.

Then the soldiers left the village, leaving the inhabitants in the blank dismay that follows a cataclysm.

"I am condemned to death," the patriarch happily repeated the rest of that day to everyone who came to console him. "I am condemned to death, my children. What charming young men they are. I am condemned to death. They are truly charming. I am condemned to death. . . ."

The death sentence hanging over the patriarch's head became more focused in the days and weeks that followed. The village, now avidly receptive to outside news in a way it had never been before, learned that the colonel and his friends, the principal architects of the April putsch, had been tried in closed court by a military tribunal. As if by design, the trial had taken place in the neighboring garrison town, in other words, in the very setting where the colonel had exerted his power. They learned that the judges had shown no mercy, although the details of the prosecution's case and the arguments of the defense were not released. The mutineers, labeled as treacherous officers, were condemned to death. There were forty-seven of them.

Their execution took place in a town quarry, which a chance excursion let me visit, a vast and sinister amphitheater located some distance away from residential areas and occupied, at one end, by a rock crusher that looked like a colossal guillotine. That was not, however, the instrument of their death.

I was told that they were led in groups of seven unfortunate men to the scene of execution. Only then, after being lined up in a row like onion plants in a vegetable patch, were their eyes covered, but they were not tied to the traditional posts. At a command from a young lieutenant and a middle-aged captain, a squad made up of bewildered young soldiers stepped forward. Without any preparation, as if everyone was anxious to be done as quickly as possible, one of the officers suddenly shouted: "Aim! Fire!"

A salvo was heard, and the seven condemned men collapsed simultaneously in a heap, like deflating dummies.

The Story of the Madman

This stage was soon over, for, when the military is thirsting for revenge, the guilt of former chiefs always seems glaringly obvious and undeserving of scrupulous hesitation. As they moved down the hierarchy of the accused, however, the debates of the military tribunal lasted longer because it seemed harder to establish the guilt of lowly subordinates when the latter pleaded ignorance of the stakes in the conflict that had swept them along and, in addition, pointed out that regulations require blind obedience of subordinates. The man in the street, uninformed about the atmosphere in the tribunal, retained only the pervading climate of revenge and extermination.

Still, although the massive executions of the first days had stopped, the newspapers continued to report from time to time that yet another mutineer had been executed after being found guilty by the military tribunal.

Then, some months later, came the turn of civilians compromised in the April putsch and the resulting regime. Some male defendants who had imprudently ventured too far were condemned and executed. For the most part, they were high-level government employees and businessmen who had made their fortunes too quickly. Only one woman suffered this deplorable fate. She had been the live-in partner of the master of the accursed regime, an agitator prone to incendiary discourse, and a businesswoman for whom no speculation was too unscrupulous.

Meanwhile, the press, television, and radio media, all under state control, had persistently been calling attention to Zoaételeu's role as mentor to the colonel, one of the highest-ranking officials of the defunct regime. They referred to him as the marabout of rebel diplomacy. Not only was he endowed with diabolical powers, they said, he was also a man of formidable intelligence entirely oriented toward perversity and egoism. At the same time that he was placing the former minister of foreign affairs under a spell through bloodcurdling methods, he had diligently raised himself from the poverty of a backward and lazy peasant to a life of the most ostentatious luxury. Teams of reporters, some equipped with cameras to take footage for television broadcast, had come to tape him, making sure not to allow him to speak and, when he did, not to report his comments. He lived in a poor hovel made of beaten earth and corrugated steel, but that was a ruse; he owned expensive furniture that had recently been confiscated by the people, and the balance in his foreign bank accounts amounted to an astronomical nest egg. "Anything goes" was apparently the motto used by pen pushers of the new leaders.

The climax of this campaign was the patriarch's arrest. One morning, the perpetual patrol of uniformed men, after slowly skirting the village going south, turned around and slowly still headed north; they parked their jeep by the side of the road, jumped out of the vehicle, and marched over to the patriarch, who was seated at his doorstep meditating on the noble lessons bequeathed by his ancestors.

"Old man, can you state your identity?" they asked.

Zoaételeu pretended not to understand; that was his favorite weapon in his resistance against the tyranny of the uniformed men.

"We want to know if you are the man whose advice led valorous officers to commit treason and who has been under house arrest as a result."

"My poor children," the old man answered, "you came to see me at least two months ago. On that occasion, you dishonored me in front of my children by asking me my name and by confiscating the tokens of a noble friendship. If you are referring to that, then yes, I am the man that you insisted on humiliating. What do you want with me this time?"

"So you are the same man? Very good. You will soon receive a visit from our colonel, who will apprise you of your fate."

In fact, the colonel commanding the neighboring garrison barged into Zoaételeu's village on the following day surrounded by his richly bedecked staff with their jutting necks, prowling fox miens, and sinister expressions, having been preceded by two troop carriers crammed with soldiers, and followed at a distance by four light armored cars and three self-propelled rocket launchers. The soldiers, in combat uniform, sprang out from under the tarpaulins as if for action and quickly formed a corridor for the great chief and his entire staff to enter the village.

Dressed in his field uniform, the colonel had barely jumped out of his vehicle when the loud and sinister roars of other military trucks made themselves heard. With the precision of a parade maneuver, they slowed to a standstill surrounding the car of the colonel commanding the neighboring garrison. Then four self-propelled rocket launchers entered and took position in the village, soon followed by a detachment of tanks whose grinding advance drove the locals to the darkest corners of their miserable, mud-walled abodes. The colonel commanding the neighboring garrison walked up to the patriarch, drew himself up, gave a military salute, and said to him, as translated by the ever more haggard and stuttering interpreter.

"Citizen Zoaételeu, in the name of the power invested in me by the people, I place you under arrest."

And the thirty-year-old scene was reenacted: despite his age, Zoaételeu was beaten and thrown unceremoniously into a jeep, after which he was spirited off as if by a whirlwind to some unknown destination.

Like thirty years earlier, nobody dared venture near the successive locales where Zoaételeu was presumably held and treated harshly to inquire about the old man's health, or, at the very least, to demand an explanation for his arrest. Old times had returned.

And, like thirty years before, Zoaételeu endured yet another calvary, for his age was worthless in shielding him from any humiliation, so resistant are the customs of such establishments to change.

He was shoved along a corridor by some people, one of whom kept hitting him and shouting, "You will have to tell us your secret, old sorcerer. We have plenty of time before your execution."

Another one cautioned, "Watch it, guys. The orders are to keep him alive and in decent shape for the execution. By order of the president. If something goes wrong, you'll answer for it. . . ."

Zoaételeu was hurled into a dark cell that reeked of urine and feces. The twenty occupants, tightly squeezed against each other and unable to stretch their legs out, had only a small metal pan that had long since overflowed and a minuscule brimming trench running diagonally across the beaten earth floor in which to relieve themselves. From time to time the door was suddenly flung open, flooding the cell with light and deafening moans that resounded relentlessly in the corridor, and which held no mystery for the old man.

The first few days he was not thrown to the torturer; he deduced rightly that he was being spared in accordance with the

The Story of the Madman

order that he be kept alive for the execution. However, mysterious events having altered the hierarchy of the country's top leaders, it quickly became apparent that the order no longer held. He was summoned before the torturer, who was a very young man, almost a boy. As he started to undress before that arguably most feared of all state employees had even had the chance to give him the order, the pleasantly surprised torturer exclaimed, "So you already know the customs of our establishment, old fetishist? And yet, you are new here."

Zoaételeu explained that he had had the honor of residing in these illustrious premises thirty years earlier, under the rule of the young man's predecessor.

"And for what reason?" roared the young man.

Zoaételeu told him his story.

"So you claim that the village idiot accused you for no reason and that you were actually innocent?" the young man sniggered. "That's what they all say. They are all innocent. And, naturally, you are also innocent of the crime of being the fetishist who inspired and advised the late colonel, minister of foreign affairs? I do not want to torture an old man, Papa, it's bad luck. My grandfather used to tell me, 'Never inflict suffering on an old man, always honor the elderly. Consider that he would curse you and then you would be lost. . . .' So, while we are alone, scream, scream loudly, scream as if I were slitting your throat, and I will strike my thigh to make it sound as if I were giving you mortal blows. Scream loudly! Scream! Howl! What are you waiting for, damned old man, sorcerer of the devil, howl! Louder!"

But the following day there was a different torturer, and Zoaételeu was treated to a good thrashing; this was the welcoming ritual, and typically, the best was yet to come.

The next day, miraculously, the young man who respected old age was back.

He said to Zoaételeu, "By the way, you remind me of someone, if I have understood the name of your village correctly. I have been thinking about it these last few days. Do you by any chance know a young man called Narcisse?"

"Narcisse?" the patriarch exclaimed. "Narcisse is my son."

The words were barely uttered when the torturer embraced him. The young man held him against his chest for a long time. Surprised, the patriarch credited the ancestors' ghosts, whose solicitude despite all appearances remained constant, for this reversal.

"But where is Narcisse?" the state employee asked.

"I have no idea," replied the patriarch.

"Thank goodness I never even scratched your venerable limbs. What a sacrilege that would have been! It must have been God himself, in his infinite mercy, who saved me from it. And what a horrible malediction would have befallen me for eternity."

At this thought, the torturer's whole body began to shake, and he fell to sobbing bitterly. He kissed the hands of the astonished old man; he dropped to his knees and kissed the patriarch's feet.

"We are related, venerable old man," the state employee continued, embracing the patriarch once more and holding him to his heart. "The blood, that sacred blood, that flows through your veins also flows through mine. What a sacrilege I would have committed! Another time, noble old man, I will tell you in detail the miraculous turns and twists that caused our blood to mix. But today, scream, scream even louder, scream as if I were slitting your throat so that I will not have to violate the holy laws of kinship by molesting the flesh of my flesh."

The following day, the torturer told the prisoner a fable that would have seemed complicated and barely intelligible to most people, but one that transported Zoaételeu to the heights of ecstasy. It was the kind of fable he loved above all else.

Women were, rightly enough, the means through which the miracle had occurred, and from what I now recall—such a long time after I was unsuccessfully initiated into these mysteries—the torturer's great grandmother was the one responsible. She had had a female child, to whom she had given birth in her father's village, before her final departure to be married. She took the child with her anyway because the infant was too young to be separated from her mother. She raised her in the husband's clan even though, according to tradition, the child belonged to her grandfather's clan, since she had been born there. However, the girl did not return to her grandfather upon reaching puberty, as she should have done, but remained with her mother, and she too, before marrying, gave birth to a male child, then to a female child, and so on. . . .

Although I was told this story thirty-six times, I am incapable of reconstituting the odyssey of these female and male children who should have gone to live with their grandfather or with their uncle according to a tradition that they all continued to defy.

It is certainly unfortunate that examining the manifestations of a passion of such importance to an entire people's soul should prove so tedious that it exposes one to the possibility of being unable to uncover the motivations behind the players' feelings, consequently giving one the sensation of being in the presence of sleepwalkers.

It is also true that the spiral of fury and madness triggered by independence created an inhuman climate that precious few were able to resist. The population of madmen that haunts the streets of our cities and who all have tragic stories similar to this one bears witness to that fact. The fathers of independence, those who first risked their lives to preach its coming, had described it to the crowds as a joyful holiday celebrating our arrival into an El Dorado. But the crowds were catapulted into a nightmare in which they are still struggling.

This professional torturer is not the least intriguing of all those sleepwalkers. Although he had no weakness for alcohol, for drugs, or for any of those plants said to be hallucinogenic, he was nevertheless prone to periods of rapture. At such times, he appeared to be under the spell of a mute exaltation. As soon as he heard the word *relative,* his gaze would focus on a far-off point as if he were having a vision in no way less fascinating than those that petrified so many Christians now canonized. The relentlessness he showed in inflicting the most excruciating pain would be transformed into a devotion capable of moving mountains.

"Your case is hopeless," he confided to the patriarch one day. "You are already condemned to die. The date of your execution has already been set. Your trial is nothing but a formality.

The Story of the Madman

You will be shot. They will tie you to the execution post; they will place the fatal blindfold on your eyes. I can already hear the officer shout the terrible command: ready, aim, fire! Your hoary skull falls to one side. Blood trickles down from the corner of your mouth; your eyes roll back; your breath turns into a hoarse death rattle. You are about to expire, venerable old man. . . ."

Terror-stricken, the torturer threw himself against the ghost-like shadows that converged on the grayish walls and drummed on them convulsively with his fists.

"It must not be," he muttered furiously. "It must not be. This cannot happen. But where is Narcisse? I must find Narcisse, my favorite schoolmate in high school, my unforgettable brother. I must."

After the fall of his benefactor, Narcisse, like so many other partisans of the overthrown regime, had taken refuge in the former colonial state, where he had lost no time in putting to use his talents as a behind-the-scenes man, immediately initiating the maneuver that would reconcile him with the new power.

He was just as anonymous here as he was everywhere else; he had never been seen in the company of the previous masters. He haunted the consulate, with Jeanne at his side. He attended the embassy's balls. His pretty companion was soon noticed by a man who was universally believed to have the ear of several ministers and probably that of the chief of state as well. This man often organized conferences for the colonies of his countrymen scattered in the large cities of the former colonial power and who were said to belong to opposition movements of a radical, not to say extremist, nature.

Narcisse and Jeanne would join these perilous expeditions, which always ended merrily in a great restaurant. Anonymous among the guests, Narcisse would discreetly confide to his nearest neighbors that the new government had remarkable qualities.

"*We* do not indulge in demagoguery like our predecessors," he would say. "*We* are responsible people. *We* only ask one thing, and that is that you judge *us* on *our* actions and not on *our* proclamations."

The Story of the Madman

His apparent self-effacement and his genuine discretion made him seem like a disinterested man. And, wonder of wonders, the radicals listened to him; they asked him questions to which he gave shallow answers that were, however, infused with a breath of enthusiasm and in which everyone could find something to support his or her own hopes or doubts.

Finally he would say, "The man who spoke to you earlier is the perfect representative of the new spirit: his good faith is genuine. Why don't you visit him from time to time? You will find that he is a countryman who is open, who is ready for a dialogue, who is brotherly. Try it. What do you have to lose?"

His influence, which for a long time remained diffused, began to manifest itself, as increasing numbers of exiles, especially those with graduate degrees who had chosen to remain abroad to defy the successive dictators, began to frequent the chancellery and the balls given by the man who was said to have the chief of state's ear. Soon, Narcisse became known to one side as an upright countryman anxious to promote national reconciliation and to the other as a passionate supporter of the regime who was all the more useful for his lack of self-interest. After all, had he not on several occasions declined offers of high-ranking positions at the embassy of the former colonial power or of other foreign capitals? There was nothing the regime would have refused him when, thanks to Osomnanga's diligence, he learned the news.

As though struck by a revelation, the delinquent finally took in the full measure of the affection his now cruelly stricken old father had borne him despite everything.

"It seems that my old man has gotten himself in a fine pickle," he confided to the man who was said to have the chief of state's ear and who was now Jeanne's protector. "Shouldn't I rush to his side? There is such a thing as filial devotion, after all. There are obligations."

"You can say that again!" his interlocutor answered. "Don't worry, I will send a dispatch. Everything will be all right, you'll see. Friends like you are not a dime a dozen these days. Even better, old friend, I have a fellow up my sleeve I highly recommend to you. This rare bird passes himself off as a lawyer, but believe me, he is mostly a pervert, a paranoid, megalomaniac exhibitionist, a sort of addict of provocation who will, in fact, end up in some buried dungeon soon. And deservedly so. But in the meantime, this lunatic can be damned useful. He has a certain talent, I'll say that much. Convince him to defend your old man and you'll see, you won't be bored. And anyway, those dinosaurs are getting on our nerves too, don't you think? Enough is enough, damn it! The twentieth century is almost over. Foreign interventions, private preserves, personal jurisdictions, one-party rule and other novelties, putsches and pronunciamentos, strongmen and orchestrated political trials, extermination of opponents and the rest of it are all very well and good, but they can't last forever. What the new generation needs is to live, my friend, truly to live, and that means modernizing. Things have got to change, finally. Do you know that every so often I can see farther than my nose, as they say? To govern is to look ahead, right? You owe me one, my brother. . . ."

Zoaételeu did not see Osomnanga, his big-hearted torturer, again. He was given over defenseless to the whims of a new specialist whom he did not know.

Every morning, for breakfast, he was made to disrobe for a long flogging session. He was brought back in the middle of the day, when people sit down to lunch, suspended from a transom with his midriff exposed and his hands and feet bound, whereupon he received caresses with which his youthful experience had fortunately familiarized him. At nightfall he was compelled to participate in even more delightful exercises.

Meanwhile, certain events that had gone completely unnoticed by common mortals had once again altered the hierarchy of the country's top leaders so that the order that he be alive and in decent shape for the execution had been reinstated and was once again in effect; he was therefore spared the bathtub he had been expecting as a deliverance, for it would surely have killed him.

After easily obtaining time off, on the pretext that the frequency of nightmare-riddled, sleepless nights he was experiencing had grown unbearable, and finding out that Narcisse was in self-imposed exile abroad, Osomnanga, the young, kind-hearted torturer, rallied Zoaételeu's clan, which he found by instinct, without once asking for directions, although he had never been there before. The villagers were still in the grip of terror, rehashing over and over the arrest and detention of the patriarch, their sacred guide. They nevertheless went about their regular chores like a herd of placid sheep who keep ruminating as disasters continue to befall them.

Aided by Zoaétoa, Narcisse's elder brother and the son most beloved by the patriarch after his younger brother, Osomnanga called together the old man's family and told them in detail the story of his kinship to them. True to custom, they welcomed his presence as a miracle. But they showed a certain inertia and skepticism when he told them that the patriarch's life was in danger and that it was possible to save him. That is not to say that they did not still love the old man to the point of veneration. It was simply that his people had resigned themselves to misfortune as was their habit, and another one of their customs so to speak.

"Let us form a delegation with the other families of the clan," he suggested. "We will go to the authorities as a crowd. We will demand that they listen; we will plead the cause of our martyr. . . ."

The day when all the families of the clan gathered together would have discouraged an ordinary man. But Osomnanga was not an ordinary man. Petty rivalries pitted groups from different villages, hamlets, generations, sexes, and even, within the same family, brothers, wives, and nephews against each other.

One patriarch bore a grudge against Zoaételeu and his children for not having visited him when he lay sick in bed for three years. Another complained that Zoaételeu and his family had not shared the fruits of the generosity of the late colonel, an assertion that was predictably passionately denied by Zoaétoa. Another opined that some people were really turning into snobs. A fourth patriarch's pretext was the disregard that Zoaételeu and his family showed for the rules of propriety traditionally observed in the clan so that the patriarch, who was today receiving his just desserts, had allegedly appropriated undeserved honors for himself during the assemblies.

The Story of the Madman

To overcome this dissent, Osomnanga was obliged to give one of those spasmodic fakir performances for which he had a knack. He strode across the square, his hands raised high over his head, his face streaming with tears. Then he lay down on the soil with his face in the dust, he pummeled the ground several times, he howled in pain, then he jumped up as if stung by a snake. Finally, he addressed the august assembly in a speech that cast those old folks into a mystical silence.

"The blood that is about to be shed," he told them, "is your blood, is our blood. A man who is a brother to some, a father to others, and a spouse to yet others, that man is going to die ignominiously. It is our own valorous blood that will be shed. How will you explain your inertia to the ancestors when you appear before them?"

As a result, a sizeable crowd went to the command headquarters of the neighboring garrison town. Still, most of the demonstrators were dragging their feet due to the anxiety in the pits of their stomachs, since they were, for the first time, participating in a rite that seemed to hold more uncertainty, not to say peril, than profit. Even Zoaétoa, usually so adventurous and hotheaded, shyly held back, milling in with the numerous laggards under the pretext that this was a job for a city man and that he himself was a man of the forest, accustomed to moving under cover.

The colonel commanding the garrison refused to see these people who were acting like rebels. He sent word to them that if they returned home, he promised to visit them any day they chose. So a date was set. Still, it was a victory, and Osomnanga's prestige grew. And it could not have come at a better time, for he had already come up against Zoaétoa's rivalry. On several occasions, the latter, posturing himself as a warrior and a man who laughed at danger, had reproached him his faint-heartedness.

The colonel commanding the neighboring garrison arrived surrounded, like the great chief he was, by the richly bedecked characters of his entire staff, with their jutting necks, not to mention their prowling fox miens, their scowling faces, and their menacing glares. He was preceded by two troop carriers crammed with soldiers and followed at a distance by four light armored cars and three self-propelled rocket launchers. The soldiers, in combat uniform, sprang out from under the tarpaulins as if for action and quickly formed a corridor for the great chief and his entire staff to enter the village.

The visitors sat down in the armchairs that had been set out for them across from the large assembly of the patriarchs of the clan. Osomnanga, ex-torturer in the capital, had orchestrated a sophisticated staging. Several patriarchs spoke, from the greenest novice to the most hoary, each putting forward a different argument, which, though generally brief, were couched in baffling rhetoric.

However, the colonel commanding the neighboring garrison, like the great chief he was, was no neophyte carried in by the latest wind. He had prepared a performance guaranteed to inspire terror along with a proper willingness for friendly submission. Being apparently unacquainted with the strategy of gradual, oblique, and circuitous encirclement, he wanted to first present himself as a thundering Jupiter before uttering politically savvy words ambiguous enough to leave the door open to all sorts of hope.

While the colonel was deploying the compact battalions of thoroughly military parlance, Osomnanga had what he considered to be an inspiration.

"Why didn't I think of it earlier?" he wondered, amazed.

"When this criminal, whom today you call your brother, your father, and your husband," the colonel concluded, "when this unworthy man was plotting against the lawful authorities, why didn't you then shower him with exhortations to moderation? Why did you not stop him? Didn't you know that the arm of the state was strong and merciless? However, take heart, citizens of this brave province; I will go cast myself, on your behalf, at the feet of the chief of state, who is our father and a magnanimous man if ever there was one. I will humbly apprise him of your request for the pardon of a criminal. The chief of state, who is our father and a magnanimous man if ever there was one, will undoubtedly retire into the seclusion of his office to ponder at length over the matter. What the verdict will be, I cannot say. But I can promise you that it will reflect the most affectionate magnanimity; it will testify to his concern for justice as well as to his love for our country and for its people."

The colonel and his staff left to the applause of the crowd, not that it was truly convinced of having been given the promise of a pardon, but rather, it had simply been seduced, as all crowds are susceptible to be, by the charm of an old soldier, that subtle mix of conqueror, father, and caricatured simpleton. A few days later, Osomnanga, assisted by a typically hot-blooded Zoaétoa, had a long uphill battle convincing the assembly of the clan of this cruel reality: nothing had been gained; quite the contrary. By all indications, the new regime was still determined to assassinate Zoaételeu. Moreover, guilty verdicts and executions continued to occur sporadically, and the hostility of the mudslingers of the government toward the elderly prisoner had not abated.

They needed to embark on a new campaign. Osomnanga was reassured by the majority that approved the broad outline he gave but soon discovered that, when it came to carrying out the plan, the old folks, as usual, dragged their feet. And yet it was this new strategy, inspired by a circumstance singular to Osomnanga, the mystique of kinship and, in this instance, a sorcerer's apprentice, that would conclusively contribute to the rescue of the patriarch.

Osomnanga knew that in the capital, among the masters, the dignitaries, the open or secret supporters, the friends, and protégés of the regime, there were several natives of the province. He promptly found out which clans they came from and organized a pilgrimage by the patriarchs to these regions.

Emissaries made a foray in a clan and by means of numerous gifts obtained a grudging endorsement from their hosts for one of those large gatherings where clans meet to exchange civilities. The throng of Zoaételeu's relatives would arrive; they were distributed throughout the area for their housing, a circumstance they would put to good use by beguiling the heads of the families they stayed with. At the very first meeting, some expert on genealogy would discover a family connection with members of the clan stricken by fate, sometimes with the entire clan. These discoveries were joyfully celebrated. With Zoaétoa's help, Osomnanga persuaded a group of elders to intercede with the powerful man who was the pride of the clan and who represented it within the chief of state's entourage. They would leave in a flurry of embraces.

And a few days later, they would make another pilgrimage to another clan, and so on. This strategy did not fail to produce results when the old man's trial finally began, all the more so because the frivolous young officer who was prosecuting the case —a protégé of the chief of state—had not studied the brief.

Narcisse flew in only a few days after the opening of the trial, which had until then consisted of an examination of Zoaételeu's character. His arrival greatly increased the confusion that had, from the start, pervaded the courtroom, where

The Story of the Madman

things were indeed not dull, as the diplomat who was the lovely Jeanne's protector had predicted. The exchanges had quickly turned into Homeric jousting between the frivolous young prosecutor and the young defense lawyer steeped in Latin and human rights, whom Narcisse had contacted by phone at the recommendation of his far-sighted friend.

"You are an old man, although no one seems to know your exact age," the frivolous prosecutor insinuated, addressing Zoaételeu. "Is it true that among your many wives there are some who are still very young?"

"My client has been subjected to the worst treatment during his detention," the defense lawyer declared. "This venerable old man, a sacred figure in our society, has been beaten, tortured, and humiliated. Isn't it time that we recognize his status as the head of his family, and his eminently venerable age? . . ."

The young jurist knew how well the worldwide campaign of demonstrations for the liberation of Nelson Mandela had awakened an awareness of human rights among his more sensitive fellow citizens. His only strategy consisted of denouncing the acts of violence committed by the regime. Educated in several Anglo-Saxon universities, he had sworn to introduce in his country defense techniques that broke from the customary stilted cowardice of his colleagues molded in the French tradition: *Fit via vi** was his motto.

"No more evasion, my dear colleague," thundered the frivolous prosecutor, who had definitely and symbolically settled for flippancy. "Is it true that this old man mates with very young women, yes or no? Where does he find the stamina? Does he not practice sorcery? That is the crux of the matter."

"Your honor," the lawyer asked the illiterate old general presiding on the bench, "how can you allow infamy to be heaped atop atrocity in this fashion?"

The presiding judge probably did not quite understand what

*Brute force made the breach (Virgil, *Aeneid* 4.494, from David West's prose translation [London: Penguin, 1991]). —*Translator's note*

The Story of the Madman

was being asked him. He turned toward his young colleague, raised an eyebrow, and resumed his hierarchical demeanor.

"Well, counselor," asked the frivolous young prosecutor, very pleased with himself, "did your client practice sorcery, yes or no? That is the crux of the matter."

"The crux of the matter, you say?" the young lawyer retorted. "The crux of the matter is that your government, your police force in this case, has no respect for anything, not even for the most venerable figure in our society: an old man whitened with age, the patriarch of a vast family. This is the crux of the matter: have you or have you not subjected this old man to unspeakable acts of violence? What is sorcery next to that? Why do you insist on brandishing this pretext? What do you know of sorcery? What does anybody know about sorcery? Nothing. . . . *Omne ignotum pro magnifico est.** Mr. Prosecutor, sorcery is a pitiful myth, a screen for fools and saboteurs. Does the court wish to place itself into one of these two categories by persisting in its obstinacy?"

Cued by imperceptible signs from the young prosecutor, the richly bedecked men who made up the court expostulated indignantly, got up, leaned over one another, broke into animated whispers, then, on a new signal from the frivolous prosecutor, meekly sat down again.

The court was far, however, from unanimously subscribing to the views of the frivolous prosecutor, and this was a result of Osomnanga's strategy. A young officer, related to an important minister who was known to be his mentor, heckled the prosecutor in the back rooms of the military tribunal.

"It is obvious what you are getting at, Commander. You want the head of this poor peasant at all costs. You are not actually going to send an old man to the firing squad on the pretext that he was the instigator of a conspiracy, are you? As a matter of fact, what do we know about it? Just between us, what do you

*Whatever is unknown is held to be magnificent (Tacitus, *Agricola* 30). —*Translator's note*

know about it? Be frank with me, Commander. What do we know about it? What do you know about it? Come on, be frank for once and live up to your rank. What do you know about it?"

"Just a moment, young man," an ally of the frivolous prosecutor protested. "There are the facts, and the facts are stubborn."

"Unfortunately, they are not the only ones," retorted the insolent young man with a knowing look, confident of the support of his protector, the minister without portfolio. "Facts may be stubborn, but so are absurd interpretations, if not more so."

During the following session, the frivolous prosecutor, who stuck to his guns when it came to carrying out his orders— given, they say, by the chief of state himself and, moreover, rendered imperative by the government-controlled media that had branded Zoaételeu the guru of the criminal putschists— remained bent on establishing that the old man was a fornicating sorcerer.

"If this man is not a sorcerer, then I'd like to know how he could have cast a spell on an entire garrison, from the simple patrol unit that, passing through the village, abandoned its equipment on the road to carouse in the village huts in full daylight instead of carrying out standard inspections, to the colonel commanding the garrison, who, after showering him with gifts, finally moved in with him."

"Are we speaking about the same man, Mr. Prosecutor?" the lawyer jeered. "So, he put a spell on a patrol unit that fell into debauchery in full daylight in the village huts, did he? This is news to us, sir. This is an aspect of the case that has been carefully kept from us. On the other hand, it has been established, and we will demonstrate it in due course, that this venerable old man, his innocence notwithstanding, was the victim of the most barbarous practices of your facilities for detention."

The public was now completely enthralled by the brilliant and courageous young man whose vituperations were cruelly lashing the military judges, not to mention the derision to which his fiery eloquence exposed them.

Poorly informed on the unexpected hazards of procedure,

The Story of the Madman

the chief of state soon called together his closest advisors to assess the gravity of the situation.

"It's a disaster," they unanimously opined.

They explained that, evidently, the young prosecutor had perused the voluminous brief too offhandedly; he did not have a firm grasp of his subject; he was the laughingstock of the enemies of the government; and the chief of state, himself, ran the very real risk of having the resulting discredit reflect on him.

Being an unimaginative man, who had, moreover, encountered nothing but submission up till then, the chief of state was ill-disposed to hearing his protégés criticized, particularly when they were members of his family. It occurred to him that the minister's faction was growing and reaching its bold tentacles even into his intimate circle.

"What do you suggest?" he asked, in order to assess the ravages caused by the invasive faction of the minister without portfolio.

"The prosecutor must be replaced and the case retried from the very beginning," the close advisors answered unanimously.

"No!" the chief of state thundered, suddenly hunched in on himself like a bulldog. "Change prosecutor? Start everything over? And what else do you want? Why not acquit the defendant right away, while we are at it? Send my nephew the following message: finish the trial, and right away. Goodnight, gentlemen!"

Finish the trial, and right away?

It was easier said than done, even for a military prosecutor under the protection of his uncle, the chief of state. It failed to take into consideration a certain tutelary and frowning authority to whom he had to give an accounting every night. Imperceptibly but surely, the political climate had changed, and the pendulum seemed about to swing in the opposite direction, as the cliché goes.

Why was the defense lawyer being so bold? And what was the cause of that arrogance, the likes of which the military prosecutor had never before encountered in his admittedly brief career? Why was he himself receiving the cold shoulder at the embassy of the former colonial power where he was now relegated to the sidelines?

The very next day, in the middle of the courtroom and during an especially stormy session of the military tribunal, the lawyer said to the prosecutor, "Mr. Prosecutor, you persist on scaling the Tarpeian rock to hoist yourself onto the roof of the Capitol, but I will continue to pull you back down to the Campus Martius, where citizens faced each other fairly. You can parade across the desolate plains of politics as much as you want, I will just as tenaciously hold tight to the ramparts of the law, which is the strength of modern nations."

The government-controlled press having foolishly reported this oratorical stroke, long lines formed the next day in front of the newsstand where they sold *Nation-Tribune,* the government daily that was usually ignored. The young lawyer's reprimands were rehashed in offices as well as in markets and on fairgrounds, and these discussions were infused with a passion usually reserved for political speeches during revolutionary times.

From where was this new wind blowing?

It apparently originated in a newspaper of the former colonial power called *L'Univers,* an evening daily, which, without sending a correspondent over, without the benefit of advice and documentation from any local corespondent, and commenting off the cuff, referred to the affair of the putschists' marabout by taking the liberty of caricaturing the political situation of the country. Accordingly, it had used the conditional tense to describe the forty-seven officers executed in a single day in a clearing. The forty-seven officers had inspired only indifference or scorn at the time, and understandably so. However, public opinion was outraged that such a serious event should be cast in doubt, and some people were even starting to say that the government of the former colonial power had undoubtedly been involved unless, in keeping with its habit of meddling in the affairs of African republics, it had itself orchestrated what was starting to be qualified in university circles as a slaughter.

On the subject of the suspicion leveled at the accused that he had resorted to mysterious expedients to satisfy the passions

The Story of the Madman

of battalions of young wives, the same daily had dared call attention to the unbridled sexuality of Africans. Finally, it had ventured an assertion that revolted the more enlightened sector of national opinion, particularly the thirty thousand students on campus. It claimed that local opposition groups—too fragmented and, furthermore, impelled either by barely understood Marxism or by anarchic instincts that were rooted in atavisms that were still unresolved despite appearances—could not be and were not, wisely enough, taken seriously.

So much cynicism and ill-natured hypocrisy had shaken the passivity of public opinion in the cities. The masses suddenly discovered what exiled intellectuals, previously branded as extremists, had been saying for years: their leaders were merely puppets whose strings were pulled by foreigners.

And that was how it all began, at least according to most of those who witnessed these events.

Instead of defusing the situation as hoped, the scorn expressed by *L'Univers* produced exactly the opposite result, further endangering the position of its protégé, the dictator–chief of state. The young lawyer's risky rhetoric easily fanned the public's jingoism, casting a new and extremely unflattering light on the government, the military tribunal, and the lies of *Nation-Tribune,* which soon stopped covering the trial completely.

It was too late. Clandestine tracts immediately took over and from then on narrated the trial in minute detail. They were so successful that soon they were sold instead of being handed out free. They acquired titles, developed an underground audience that impatiently awaited their release, and, spurred by competition, strove to outdo each other in prowess, in reporting original stories, in denouncing forgotten or recent crimes, and in offering unique features.

Debout l'Afrique, the first one to appear, was so popular it caused riots. There was *Liberté, Liberté . . . ,* which was the first to report on the wealth accumulated abroad by political leaders and members of the administration, and especially by the chief of state. There was *Afrique-Libération,* the first to be published on a regular schedule, an occurrence that was, according to the lawyer steeped in human rights, as decisive as the crossing of the Rubicon by the conquerors of Gaul. There was *L'Indépendant,* a champion of outrageously ultranationalist themes with xenophobic overtones; it was the first to expose thoroughly and in a well-documented way the shady business dealings between the chief of state and the eldest son of the president of the former colonial power. There was *L'Avenir,* the first to regularly provide a venue for the unemployed, for bankrupt people, for students, for illicit street vendors, and even for prostitutes because, it claimed, the interests of all the children of the nation should have equal weight. There was *Le Provocateur,* whose diabolical trump card was a superb artist who soon specialized in caricatures of the chief of state, for which the public developed an appreciative appetite. There was *Jeunesse Joyeuse,* or *J.J.* as its fanatical public liked to call it. Examinations, certificates, and various secondary and specialized diplomas were both its specialty and its mother lode. *Jeunesse Joyeuse* supplied honest advice on how to succeed, speculative reports on current issues, but also tried and true techniques for cheating or for outwitting the examining supervisor when the candidate was a young woman or the target a male.

There were many more publications, most of which disappeared after a brief run.

The police forces of the regime did not fail to unleash their fury against this clandestine press, arisen spontaneously from Zoáételeu's saga, but they displayed a lack of coherence in their repressive campaign. Sometimes they would look the other way, giving rise to speculations that the chief of state, under pressure from the former colonial power, which claimed to be urging African dictators to moderation, and from his friends and protégés, might finally have resigned himself to the triumph of free speech. Then, suddenly, completely out of the blue, police goons would seize newspapers, destroy presses, and either flog the avowed journalists or throw them in jail. A half dozen members of this noble if unfortunate company, who had walked into the various locales of the forces of order, never came out again, or else came out feet first.

The Story of the Madman

However, the combative spirit of the writers did not flag but rather grew.

One of these papers dared to write openly that, should it prove true that a poor peasant had been kidnapped from his village, locked up in filthy quarters, beaten, tortured, and humiliated, as his lawyer claimed, then it should be the treacherous officers of the military tribunal and the corrupt leaders of this puppet regime who should be tried immediately and condemned to hang without delay, including, obviously, the worst offender, the chief of state.

As the expression goes—and the image is very appropriate in this case—the tensions continued to mount. The prosecutor informed the tribunal, which was now meeting behind closed doors, of his decision to close the debate in order to allow the court to start its deliberations. The defense lawyer cried foul, threatened to persuade his client to go on a hunger strike, promising to join him. The clandestine newspapers jubilantly reported this development to the public. The BBC discovered the story of the so-called guru of the putschists and issued frequent reports on the subject in its information bulletins transmitted on the African continent.

"What do you advise me to do?" the chief of state asked his row of close advisors, who were summoned daily.

"Let us cut our losses," they unanimously replied. "It is our only way out. Your Excellency, release this man and you will be praised for centuries to come as the most generous chief of state and a real democrat, the first on the African continent."

"Go on," thundered the chief of state. "Keep reciting that lawyer's speeches back to me: the clemency of Augustus will not hold a candle to the magnanimity of the chief of state. . . . Isn't that what he said just yesterday? The clemency of Augustus . . . if only I knew who the devil that was. The clemency of Augustus. I knew from the start that you would eventually ask me to acquit that monster. I tell you that he is the one behind the April putsch. The others were just wimps! It would never have occurred to them to oust me. There must have been an external catalyst, a certain something, a . . . I don't know. . . . It was him. I tell you that it was him. Send word to my nephew that, by order of the chief of state, the case is closed. . . ."

"That's impossible," they answered in unison. "It can't be done without first acceding to the lawyer's request. Otherwise, no one will be able to answer for the consequences."

"And just what does he want now?"

"He wants to call a witness, a young man who has just returned from abroad and who claims to be the defendant's son."

"All right, I will allow this new testimony," the chief of state growled, hunched in on himself like a bulldog, "but this will be the last session of this masquerade, is that clear? I want each of you to answer me. Is that quite clear this time?"

"Quite clear, Your Excellency," the first close advisor answered, bowing.

"Quite clear, Your Excellency," the second close advisor answered, bowing.

"Quite clear, Your Excellency," the third close advisor answered, bowing.

"Quite clear, Your Excellency," the fourth close advisor answered, bowing.

"Quite clear, Your Excellency," the fifth close advisor answered, bowing.

"Quite clear, Your Excellency," the sixth close advisor answered, bowing.

"Quite clear . . ."

"All right, all right," the chief of state interrupted, almost reassured. "You know what you have to do. Go on, get out of here. . . ."

THE DAY NARCISSE appeared in front of the military tribunal, which was now meeting behind closed doors, marked a major turn in public opinion at the expense of the military tribunal and of the regime.

It became particularly obvious, to the dismay of the authorities, that the crowd was no longer afraid of confronting the arsenal of police violence or that of any other group resembling it—the army, the national police, militias, and volunteer guardians of order. Truncheon blows, charges by policemen with shields, fire hoses, tear gas, and even the lobbing of standard grenades could not disperse the ever growing crowds that gathered at dawn around the location of the military tribunal.

Nothing worked until the arrival of helicopters flying in formation—manned, I was told, by white pilots, who were Israelis, according to some, French, according to others—which grazed the crowd in order to sow panic and disperse it.

The miraculously well-informed clandestine newspapers did not fail to give a very detailed and accurate account of the new confrontation between the titans of the courtroom. Once again, the prosecutor won hands down the medal for frivolity and nonchalance.

"How is it," he thundered at Narcisse during the identification interrogation, "that you do not bear the name of the man you claim is your father?"

Without raising his voice, the lawyer objected, "The prosecutor's studies abroad have obviously kept him out of the country for too long; as a result he has forgotten the ways and customs of our people. Doesn't the prosecutor know that, in our culture, it is not customary to name the son after the father?"

"There are forty-five of us male children sired by our father," Narcisse stated confidently, "and we all have different names, just as each tree in our forests bears its own name. Nature, the mother of us all, has set the example."

Questioned about the sexual practices attributed to his father by the prosecution, Narcisse, who now spoke with the accent of the former colonial power in which he had recently resided, gave that formidable reply that conclusively discredited the regime.

"Only perverts, lunatics, sexual maniacs, or psychopaths could have come up with such self-demeaning nonsense. Although I am not a doctor, I am educated enough to be able to state categorically that all of my septuagenarian father's wives have reached menopause."

"Are you saying that your father is not in the habit of sharing his bed with young women?" the lawyer asked, to drive the point home.

"What young women?" Narcisse protested. "The only young women in the village are his sons' wives, in other words, his daughters-in-law. It is true that they are legion; our father likes to saddle us with wives without consulting us. I tell you, if I had not put my foot down, I would already have five or six. What can I say, his passion is to smother us with wives and to count his progeny daily the way others count their cows, their sheep, or their gold coins. This is where he sinks his meager income and his immense prestige as a wise man. You could say that my venerable father is the Harpagon of progeny. The only young women at home are ours. If anyone attempts to insinuate that this noble old man has intimate knowledge of his daughters-in-law, who would believe such a sacrilege? Who, besides a lunatic, could conceive of such a repulsive thought? Since my father, whom you have not deigned to address in his own language, cannot defend his honor himself, I would like, here and now, to state my disgust, gentlemen of the court."

I have been able to establish, conclusively for my purposes, that this last speech had been entirely dictated to Narcisse by the lawyer; moreover, he recited it perfectly, overcoming his agora-phobia for once. Zoaétoa witnessed the scene; it made him so proud that, for the first time, he was able to accept the prefer-ence demonstrated by his father for Narcisse, whom he had con-sidered a brat until then.

Asked by the prosecutor to explain the bond that had united two such dissimilar beings as the patriarch and the late colonel, Narcisse replied with some arrogance: "That is where you are greatly mistaken, Mister Prosecutor. My father and the colonel were not so different. First of all, they were both what we call in our vernacular native sons, two men bred in the same region, our own, shaped by the same age-old traditions, both aspiring to the same happiness and the same solidarity. That is what a native son is, Mister Prosecutor. Furthermore, my father is a wise man, an experienced, thoughtful, and patient man. As for the colonel, he was a relentless seeker of truth; he was a kind of researcher, a scholar; he wanted to uncover the mysteries of our culture; like my father, he was a lover of tradition. He became fascinated by this noble old man from their very first meeting."

"And what were the circumstances of this meeting?" the law-yer rashly inquired, forcing Narcisse to improvise for the first time.

"Well," Narcisse continued, clearing his throat. His head was still full of the rhetoric he had been exposed to at the meetings in the former colonial metropolis. "Well, actually, it was mainly by chance that it occurred. Are there any limits, gentlemen, to what chance can accomplish? Well, here goes, I will tell you all about it. It's very simple. A patrol was forced to park its jeep near our village to fix a flat tire. Yes, indeed, this is how it all started, you can take my word for it. Now, it so happened that the colonel passed by, unexpectedly, on his way back from an inspection tour, you see. He saw his men bustling around the jeep with that sense of discipline and initiative that character-izes our humble privates when they are competently led. The colonel, moved by this scene—as I can attest, having seen it with my own eyes—stopped his limousine, unaffectedly stepped out of his car, took an active interest in their task to encourage them along, and passed out cigarettes and beer. Suddenly, look-ing up to take in his surroundings, he saw my father, who was seated at his doorstep peacefully chatting with his grandchil-dren. This scene dazzled the colonel, who was a peace-loving dreamer."

"This is a scandal!" sputtered the prosecutor. "You dare praise that criminal who was justly sentenced by a military tri-bunal, with the unanimous approval of the people, to face a firing squad? A scandal. . . ."

"How am I supposed to know," Narcisse retorted triumphantly, encouraged by a wink from the lawyer. "How am I supposed to know; you ask me a question, I answer. What is the problem? Shouldn't I have answered?"

The frivolous prosecutor bid the illiterate old general pre-siding on the bench to declare a recess. The illiterate old gen-eral complied. The court retired to consult among themselves. Clutching this pretext as a dog would a bone, the prosecutor contended that this provocation justified putting an end to the debates, which had lasted too long as it was.

"How can we do that?" countered the argumentative young captain, bolstered by the support of a minister without port-folio. "You want the head of that poor old man, we all get the picture. But we must still respect proprieties, sir."

His argument prevailed. The prosecutor had to give in, al-though he did so ungraciously.

When the session resumed, the lawyer, who had also con-sulted with his client, presented the latter's excuses to the court claiming that it had not been Narcisse's intention to question the authority or the sagacity of the military judges. The court seemed satisfied by the extremely conciliatory tone of this state-ment.

The damage was done. Insolence was no longer the prerog-ative of clandestine newspapers; it had contaminated the man in the street, and Narcisse pontificating in front of the military tribunal was living proof of it.

Deeply discouraged, the prosecutor forgot to ask Narcisse the one question that, he had been told, could not fail to embarrass the young man. It concerned the origin of his wealth as well as the nature of his relationship with Jeanne. By some fatality, the prosecutor, who was excessively emotional and impulsive, continued to stress an aspect of the case that he had failed to study properly and which, by causing him to stumble, betrayed his superficiality. On the other hand, in the areas where the police investigation had provided him with deadly ammunition, he was unable to drive his easy advantage home due to an unforeseen circumstance of the case.

Narcisse would have been hard put to account for his current fortune, especially since it dated from only a few months back. Although the same could be said of a large number of citizens, on whom the police force—not very competent and, furthermore, overwhelmed and little inclined to be zealous given the uncertainty of the future—was incapable of conducting thorough investigations. Yet the chronological coincidence between Narcisse's enrichment and the April putsch was glaring. Once cornered on this issue, the delinquent's recently acquired loquacity would certainly not have been enough to save him. The same could have been said about Jeanne and her past intimacy with the late colonel.

The prosecutor proved incapable of using to his advantage the files that an uncharacteristically perspicacious and diligent police force had gathered in a few days on those two individuals. Away from the parades, the cocktail parties, and the balls that had previously been the staple of its existence, the small world of the power elite felt as though it had been swept up in a tornado and was floundering. The public was in stitches over its confusion. Time was passing. Osomnanga, fanatically, pressed on with his pilgrimages. Zoaételeu was still alive. The chief of state was still determined to finish the trial, and right away.

"Put an end to this right away!" he kept mumbling in the privacy of his office and of his living quarters, as he feverishly paced the floor.

The chief of state finally reluctantly convened what can only be called his family council, a veritable den of hawks who preached war for every problem. They daily admonished him that, to be a leader, one had to have substance, daring, courage, nerves, determination, firmness, and follow-through.

"Is it by chance that you are where you are?" they asked. "Providence itself willed it thus. Providence is mysterious; its ways are impenetrable. It chose you to be the leader; you are the leader; be a leader. You must make decisions and act like a leader."

Cornered, the chief of state had consequently resigned himself to complying with the wishes of his terrible family. Nevertheless, he chose to speak in veiled terms, and they all understood his meaning explicitly.

"It is time to act," he said cryptically. "The paths taken until now have led nowhere. The time has come for new methods. I want this matter resolved, is that clear? Let's get it over with right away—that is my will."

"What we lose in deterrence we will make up in expeditiousness," agreed the frivolous young prosecutor with a vengeance to satisfy. "We must respect formalities, however. Formalities are everything, as my colleagues in the military tribunal keep telling me."

"But isn't it risky?" worried the father of the chief of state's youngest concubine.

"What risk?" the uncle of the chief of state and the last surviving member of his generation demanded to know.

"Risk?" exclaimed the chief of state's eldest brother, a virtuoso of fraudulent banking transactions. "There are no risks. The International Monetary Fund and the World Bank, not to mention the minister of finance and the minister of cooperation of the former colonial power, have placed their trust in us. These institutions and high-ranking officials have demonstrated their friendship to us. They will never abandon us, whatever happens."

"Is that really certain?" the chief of state wondered uneasily, recalling the recent troubles of his fellow leaders in other francophone countries. "What does our deputy secretary at the embassy in Washington think?"

"Openly or covertly, the leaders there are behind us, just like those of the former colonial power. We can be sure of that," opined the deputy secretary at the embassy in Washington, who happened to be the chief of state's younger brother. "Still, we must watch out for the American human rights organizations, which are formidable outfits, for, once they are unleashed, nothing can stop them, not even their own president. If word of the accident should get out, their leaders will probably demand an investigation by an international commission."

"No word of the accident will get out," peremptorily responded the chief of the gendarmerie, who was the son of a first cousin of the chief of state's. "I will see to it personally, leave it to me. It is a standard operation that must be carried out as simply as possible. There are several equally easy options open to us. First, there is an escape attempt in collusion with a corrupt guard. I already have one up my sleeve, ready to be used. . . ."

"Spare the chief of state the details, will you?" interrupted the prosecutor, who was frivolous but savvy in criminal law.

"What other major point can we settle together?" the chief of state asked, once again speaking in veiled terms and, in a way, coming to his dear nephew's rescue anew.

"We must ensure that the public accept the accident as such," pointed out the editor-in-chief of *Nation-Tribune,* the eldest son of the chief of state's youngest sister and a recent graduate of a foreign school of journalism. He was also the head of the presidency's press office. "Personally, I suggest that the accident take place during a medical procedure. The advanced age of the individual in question will give credibility to our indignant protests, along with threats of prosecution against any possible malicious insinuations."

"During a medical procedure! That's an excellent idea," opined the chief of state.

"But the personnel at the university hospital are fairly worked up," stated the minister of health, an *agrégé* in medicine* and, incidentally, the chief of state's eldest brother. "Most of our employees are from ethnic groups that are hostile to us."

---

*A person who has passed the competitive examination conducted by the French state, qualifying the candidate to teach at the secondary level (*lycée* or *collège*). The minister of health's *agrégation* in medicine is a self-proclaimed degree.— *Translator's note*

"But that was the best solution," the chief of the gendarmerie protested.

"I am aware of that. But given the nature of my responsibilities, which I freely assume, I had to call that situation to your attention," the *agrégé* in medicine answered.

"There is another possibility that no one seems to have thought of yet," said the second husband of the chief of state's only maternal aunt, a self-professed doctoral candidate in applied psychology from the University of Rouen* and, despite his advanced age, the head of that department at the National University. "This man is of a canonical, not to say biblical, age. People described him as a septuagenarian, but that's not certain. He might be an octogenarian or even a nonagenarian. At his time of life, the heart is so frail, a strong shock is all it takes."

"Here is what I call a fertile, and even a brilliant, imagination," the chief of state immediately and boastfully exclaimed, speaking openly at last. "Gentlemen, take a good look at what you see standing before you: this is a resourceful man. Go on, Mr. Psychologist, this is very interesting."

"Well," continued the psychologist, "instead of the prisoner himself having an accident, an occurrence that might give rise to suspicion, why not pick a close relative instead, some insignificant character whose sudden death would invite no speculation? However, on hearing the news, the interested party would suffer a fatal shock."

"A fatal shock!" the prosecutor, with a vengeance to satisfy, repeated with conviction. "That would certainly settle our problem. Fatal shock it is, then. I enthusiastically vote for the fatal shock solution. There is a problem, however. If I understood correctly, the prospective victim of our accident must be both insignificant and dear to the subject's heart."

"Exactly," the psychologist replied.

"That's a little like a five-legged sheep, isn't it?" the frivolous prosecutor sneered.

"Yeah, it's not a bad idea," the chief of state concluded. "In fact, it's an excellent idea. So be it."

---

*And yet, to my knowledge, he lived in Rouen a total of only two short weeks. — *Author's note*

However, the doctoral candidate in applied psychology from the University of Rouen still had something to add:

"To be methodical about this, we must still consider the potential of failure and its resulting consequences. I emphasize this only in the interest of the right method; we cannot leave without considering the possibility of failure and the resulting consequences. It would be very imprudent to do so, and besides, it would not be methodical. I insist on this; I'm a methodical man."

The resourceful psychologist's suggestion threw a sudden chill on the family gathering. Although the talents in this group flourished more each day, as has been the case in the entire republic since its triumphant entry into the congress of nations, according to the official newspapers at any rate, the cultivation of foresight has been sadly neglected.

The members of this particular envied social circle, like those of other social circles of the republic in fact—but, in the latter, with no particularly harmful consequences to the nation —prized above all else the gift of intuition, and those who possess it, those who are spontaneous, impulsive, not to mention their colleagues, the improvisers of all stripes, all as privileged heroes of divinity. The people, in fact, who know everything without having learned anything, who proudly hold the highest offices without any qualifications for their tenure, who settle vital issues and cut Gordian knots with no particular competence for the job, who scorn both theory and practice, and who fly to the dizzying heights of destiny without having received the call to greatness.

And it was one of these men beloved of the gods, a king of intuition, who dazzlingly lifted the family out of the confusion created by the imprudent suggestion of the resourceful psychologist. He had arrived last, when the family council was already well under way and had until then stayed out of the discussion, not from a conscious choice dictated by a seemly reserve borne out of deliberate circumspection, but rather because he was still in the fog of receding inebriation.

In a family in which titles and qualifications clinked against each other ceaselessly like so much pocket change, this man had no title other than that of being the chief of state's eldest son.

He had no qualifications besides a baccalaureate degree, section A (with only one modern language)—and, in order for him to finally obtain that coveted diploma, this priceless character had had to be removed from a private school in the former colonial nation after five successive failures and be repatriated *manu militari,** for he liked it very much over there, to present him for examination by a national jury whose members had, on the previous night, dined in the ceremonial rooms of his father's palace.

He had finally awakened at the point when the psychologist was explaining his fatal emotion tactic and had recognized its merits, just like his illustrious sire, the chief of state, whose instantaneous approval his son had not failed to fully appreciate. And now the last contribution from the resourceful psychologist, which had confounded and discomfited the gathering, gave him an opening to make a brilliant entrance into the arena.

"In case of failure?" he articulated cheerfully. "Well, my friends, should we fail, all we have to do is try again with another victim, of course! One should be consistent when dealing with peasants. Why should we rack our brains over it? We'll just start again, that's all."

This advice, which deserves to go down in the annals of the republic, was unanimously admired and applauded, and the meeting came to an end.

All that was left to do was to put the diabolical plan into action, and the resourceful psychologist immediately nominated himself as overseer, while enlisting the services of all his regular and backup collaborators in important endeavors.

As a result of this highly eventful family gathering, a very unusual occurrence took place in Zoaételeu's village a few days later.

*By force. —*Translator's note*

ONE AFTERNOON, around the time when the downcast inhabitants of the patriarch's village were starting to file back from the forest, two white RVs bearing the inscription "Mobile Hygiene and Preventative Care" in bright red letters parked next to each other by the side of the road. Several young women, students from the applied psychology department at the National University, trooped out together and, arm in arm, crossed the village square and entered into conversation with the villagers.

Dressed in sparklingly white shirts and caps of the same color but wearing small red crosses on their foreheads, they claimed to be nurses. They were attractive and pleasant, engaging even. They emanated a heady and insistent perfume about them.

They explained that the Red Cross, appalled and outraged by the news of the unjustifiable detention of the patriarch and by all their other misfortunes, had sent them, in keeping with its charitable mission, to relieve the villagers' suffering as much as possible. They would stay in the village a few weeks to nurse the sick and the children. In addition, they would use that time to draw up a list of various injustices suffered by their new protégés. The humanitarian organization pledged to file a complaint with the international courts in order to put an end to these abuses and, while they were at it, to demand reparations.

The community, whose leadership Zoaétoa had recently usurped, gave the intruders a sullen and faintly hostile reception.

"Don't worry," they told the villagers over and over, "the foreign humanitarian organization, whose missionaries we are, will protect you efficiently, if only from a distance. Before anyone can touch a hair on your heads, they will first have to trample over our dead bodies and brave the renowned might of the Red Cross, in front of whom all world governments bow, without exception."

The supposed nurses wasted no time settling in and getting organized. The very next day, they put up a tent in the village square, and daily at dusk, when the peasants had returned from the forest, they would see both children and adult patients whom they picked from among the two or three families they had just visited.

At nightfall, the young women repaired to their vehicles, which were apparently equipped to provide for their shelter. The rest of the time, that is to say most of the day, they dwelled among the peasants like fishes in water. The resourceful psychologist, the doctoral candidate in applied psychology from the University of Rouen, was truly a methodical man, as he himself liked to say.

When some poor mother, returning from the fields, entered the square with a heavy basket on her back and her baby hanging at her breast, the pseudo-nurses rushed to relieve her of part of her load. If a small child had a ballooning stomach, they sought its father's permission to administer a vermifuge. If a peasant, in his endless battle against the invasion of the forest, cut his finger, his leg, or his arm, they applied cream on the wound and dressed it. If, as often happened, a group of barechested young men nonchalantly headed toward the river with old washcloths in one hand and back scrubbers in the other, they eagerly offered to accompany them. If some of the inhabitants complained about the destitution that had afflicted them since the patriarch's deportation, they drove their RVs to the neighboring garrison town and brought back a generous supply of beer, cigarettes, cases of table wine, dried fish, bags of rice, and other similar food. Whatever the nature of the wound and however advanced its progression, the pseudo-nurses always found some balm to pour on it.

An old woman died; the deeply distressed pseudo-nurses donated a pine coffin. They brought back from the neighboring

The Story of the Madman

area a white-haired missionary, the revered as well as renowned founder of a large number of proselytizing establishments, who was on the verge of retirement. The religious man with the long white beard piously accompanied the dead woman to her last resting place. Although religions in any way hostile to the free multiplication of men and women were rarely welcomed in the land of the unfortunate patriarch, this act of devout generosity, ennobled moreover by the somber gravity of a rite that delighted the peasants, completely conquered those simple-hearted souls.

Afterward, the pseudo-nurses thoughtlessly hired a mason, who erected a modest but admirable construction, the likes of which had, besides, never been seen in the province, on the tomb of the deceased. From that point on, they were ascribed with miraculous powers and attracted all the unhappy souls longing for miracles. The lame accosted and beseeched them; the paralyzed had themselves placed in their path; sterile women asked them to place their hands on their unhappy foreheads. The time had come to move to the next phase.

Hadn't they, after all, conclusively demonstrated their independence from the government as well as their sincere affection for these oppressed peasants? The perennial patrol of uniformed men had frequently stopped in the village and jumped out of its vehicle with that ferociously martial air that characterized it, to subject the strangers to a routine inspection but with meticulous zeal. Their papers were apparently in order, and each time the manifestly disappointed and downcast patrol would have to give up and leave, though somewhat ungraciously, seemingly dejected by the persistent administrative correctness of these undesirable and untouchable persons.

So, the pseudo-nurses called together the villagers and asked them to state their grievances. The male villagers, who were an exalted lot, did not need much encouragement and proceeded with the airing they were being invited to do. Each time one of them stood up to speak, the attractive young women would ask, "What is your name? How are you related to the jailed patriarch?"

They feverishly noted down the answers given by the speaker

in their record books, ostensibly along with the complaints the villagers were articulating. These sessions lasted two long days, during which time the so-called nurses of the Red Cross were amply able not only to determine the precise kinship of everyone to the unfortunate patriarch but also to survey the inhabitants of the village.

That night, gathered together in one of the trailers around the record books, where they had noted thousands of pieces of information, they did an initial sifting as they had been instructed to do. And that was when, after hanging in the balance, the patriarch's destiny was sealed. Had any of the villagers spied on the young women—as Zoaétoa had briefly contemplated doing but was unfortunately too intimidated by the city creatures to dare—he would have been unable to recognize in this spectacle of mixed frivolity, vileness, and the most abject servility, the creatures who were generally believed to be angels from heaven. And yet those were the traits usually displayed by civil servants after thirty years of being kneaded like clay and finally dehumanized by dictatorships.

"I nominate as the subject of our . . . let us say, our experiment, the first wife of the old schmuck. She must be at least sixty or sixty-five," the first pseudo-nurse proposed.

"Why her?" the others asked. "What a ridiculous idea!"

"Because the first person we fall in love with is always the one who remains closest to our heart," she answered.

"Fiddlesticks," one of her friends retorted. "That's what you think, or rather, that's what women think. It's not the same for men. And besides, it's easy for you to say, 'love.' What is love anyway? Especially here?"

"Besides," continued another, "our friend here is mistaken; his real first love, the one he married first, died in labor giving birth to the old fool's eldest son. The one our friend is referring to took the place of the deceased. She is not the actual first wife. I nominate the favorite wife."

"How," sneered all the others, "did you manage to spot the favorite?"

"Oh, it was easy. She has a cute face, and besides, she is the youngest. Old men love the young ones," she answered.

"This hypothesis is too obscure!" the others objected. "Besides, why are we only interested in women? Why not men? Why not the eldest son? They say that his birth produces the most wonderful emotion parents ever feel, especially for the father. He is the child they stake the most on, the one they are proudest of. What a heartbreak if he were to die in his prime!"

"Doesn't the same reasoning apply to the youngest—I mean the youngest son, of course?" a very young and particularly eloquent pseudo-nurse objected. "Wouldn't he inspire the most tenderness? There will be no more children after him. He is like a living warning of approaching old age, if not death. His passing would be the one to cause a mortal shock."

"I have another idea," offered a nurse who had been silent until then. "By chance, I was able to learn some things that will surprise you. Among the old lunatic's many children, there is one he loves more than any of the others. Guess who it is."

"You are going to tell us," the others answered in unison. "You are the one chance smiled upon, not us, you simp!"

"It's Narcisse."

"The pretentious one who returned from exile to testify at the trial? So?"

"But Narcisse has been a continuous heartbreak to his father. He is what you might call a rebel. His father adored him no less because of it. Finally, after endless stratagems and accommodations, the old man managed to get him to accept the fiancée he had chosen for him."

"So?"

"Guess what happened. . . ."

"He impregnated her? It's obvious. It's the only thing the men around here know how to do. So?"

"Doesn't a favorite son sire an idolized grandson? And wouldn't that grandson's birth be eagerly awaited? And what would be the effect of a brutal deception after this eager anticipation? You don't answer? And yet it's simple. The brutal interruption of eager anticipation produces a fatal shock, don't you see?"

"Where is this girl?" her listeners asked in unison.

"Right here, in the village!"

The Story of the Madman

"Is she beautiful?"

"She is hideous, horrible!" the young woman replied laughing. "She is a monster. She looks like a cross between an orangutan and the abominable snowman, anyway she is something unspeakable. She is an absolute nightmare, I tell you, an absolute nightmare."

The pseudo-nurses pinched themselves in disbelief and stared at each other wide-eyed as if to convince themselves that they were not dreaming.

They left the village promising to return soon.

They reported the results of their mission to the head of the department of applied psychology at the National University, who, as they had expected, did not congratulate them, since he never congratulated anybody. On the contrary, he went to great lengths to convince them that the unorthodox methods they had used to approach the problem and to conduct the investigation had flaws which, according to him, obliterated whatever possible value the results they had obtained might have had. He then curtly dismissed them before going to see the minister of health, an *agrégé* in medicine.

"Your Excellency," he said. "Our girls have done an excellent job, in my opinion; they have not only happened on a good thing; they have, in addition, made recommendations that are also quite felicitous, and I strongly recommend them to you."

The minister of health, an *agrégé* in medicine, summoned to his office that very night two young women doctors who had learned some useful lessons from specialists on loan from a foreign embassy.

"You know what you have to do. Carry out your orders. And most important, once you are there, you must look like a team to the peasants; even more than that, you must look like a seamlessly united and happy family."

When they set foot in the village again, with three RVs this time, the young nurses were under the command of the two young women doctors, who did nothing, however, to distinguish themselves from their companions but rather attempted to blend into the group instead.

On the day they arrived, the team, having set up shop in a

The Story of the Madman

tent in the middle of the village, proceeded to vaccinate all the children of the small community. But as soon as night fell, the pseudo-nurses, flanked by the women doctors, lured Narcisse's little fiancée into one of the RVs. They asked her how long she had been pregnant.

"I don't know," the poor girl cried, bursting into tears.

"Are you happy?" asked the city women.

"No," she answered impetuously, without really understanding the question.

With the charming naiveté typical of pregnant adolescents, she confided to them her despair at being separated from the love of her life and at having received no sign of affection from him for many long months.

"Can you at least tell me whether he is still alive?" she asked them frantically.

"Don't you worry, my girl," they told her, "you will see him again soon as if by magic, and he will hold you in his arms as he has never done before. We have here a magic potion that will bring your man back to you, you'll see. Just do exactly as we say and happiness will soon be yours."

They gave her some pills and an intravenous injection. The following day, at nightfall, they again lured her to an RV and repeated the process.

The next day, confident of having assassinated the fetus, an abominable crime if ever there was one—compelled by that despicable folly to dominate men known as politics—these women took their final leave from the village of the unfortunate patriarch without so much as a twinge of remorse.

THE YOUNG CAPTAIN from the military tribunal, suddenly turning bolder, as if he had been struck by an inspiration, sought a meeting with Narcisse's lawyer, despite the fact that the latter was anathema to high military officials and had previously been vilified on every possible occasion by him.

"In this case, at any rate, we are on the same side," the captain told the lawyer, convinced that he was doing him an honor or reassuring him. "Let us join forces."

"My dear captain," the young lawyer answered, "I must own that I am skeptical, not to say suspicious. Your kind does not usually fight for human rights. Why don't you tell me your real motives? What is going on? Is your representative, the minister, preparing an umpteenth coup? In other words, aren't you planning to use me to advance goals that I disapprove of? I have no sympathy for the military, as everyone knows, since I have said it often enough. So exactly what do you want with me?"

"You place me in an awkward position, Counselor," the captain answered. "I have not been authorized to reveal our motives to you."

"In that case, don't count on me. Good-bye."

"Wait, Counselor, please wait. You really are placing me in an awkward position. I have to consult my friends."

"Your friends? You mean the minister?"

"Well, yes. I can't tell you anything without first consulting the one you call the minister."

"And who is, in fact, your father from the wrong side of the sheets, as they say in the West?"

"That's correct. You are well informed, Counselor. How do you do it?"

"That, my dear friend, is my secret. Well, spit it out; what are you driving at? You are planning a new coup and you want to use me as a safety card? We know all about your kind. Your intentions are always low; you are criminals. You don't care about people or the country. Those are empty words for you. You are conniving with the former colonial power, which also considers Africa a mere abstraction it can juggle, like an acrobat on the stage of international politics. You are its trump card, in fact. You should not always take us for such complete asses. When things get really bad and we can no longer extricate ourselves from that sea of shit the juggler keeps refilling, and it will not be long now, he will perform another tour de force—he will miraculously pull you out of his hat and long live international cooperation! Isn't that it? We too know all about politics on the grand scale."

"Listen, meet me here tomorrow, at this same time. By then, I may have been authorized to tell you everything. It is much simpler than you think, much more intrinsic to our culture. You would be surprised if I opened my soul to you."

"Open it then, what are you waiting for? What's the problem?"

"Meet me here tomorrow, at this same time. I promise you that you will be amazed when you find out how simple it is. Come with your client, Narcisse. I think I can promise to have convinced the minister to let me confide in you."

The next day, the young captain was indeed prompt to arrive.

"Well," he said to the lawyer, and simultaneously including Narcisse, who had accompanied the latter, in the conversation, "finally, I will tell you everything; I have obtained permission to do so."

"How fortunate," commented the lawyer, who was always, a priori, hostile toward representatives of the establishment.

Turning to Narcisse, the captain asked, "Can I call you Narcisse, since we are related? Did you know that we are related?"

"No," Narcisse answered noncommittally.

"Well, I'm telling you, man, we're related; that's what I've been told."

"Who told you so? The minister?" the lawyer asked.

"Precisely," answered the captain. "I'm just repeating what I have been told. Narcisse must have heard of a certain Zambo Menduga, right?"

"Yes . . . maybe," Narcisse replied hesitantly.

"But have you also heard of a certain Mani Akamseu?"

"Not really. Wait a minute . . . that sounds vaguely familiar. I do believe that I have heard my old man mention that name. Yes. . . ."

"You must also have heard about the crossing of the river. Apparently, it took place at night. There was a monstrous snake that stretched across the river allowing our people to cross over on this makeshift bridge. Have you perhaps heard this before? This strange story was a refrain throughout my childhood."

"Well, yeah, you know, maybe, certainly . . . When the old folks start rambling, I just listen with one ear. When it comes to rambling, they can really go at it with all those stories. You can't live on these stories, you know."

"Don't you believe it, my brother," the captain said. "Because to the old folks, they are not stories but reality, or rather history. But to get back to the subject: so, after only a portion of our people had crossed over, some clumsy oaf, in his haste, dropped a burning coal on the snake's back. Stung by the burn, the enormous reptile dove into the river."

"So then?" asked the fascinated lawyer.

"Some of our people were not able to cross and remained, in effect, prisoner on the other bank. Mani Akamseu and Zambo Menduga were two brothers who were the leaders of the two clans. Your clan, that of Zambo Menduga, crossed the river. We, the descendants of Mani Akamseu, remained behind."

"Yes, I have heard that story," Narcisse said. "But it sure sounds like a fable, if it isn't one."

"Well, my dear fellow, apparently it is our history, yours and mine."

The lawyer, who was an enlightened man, grew suddenly afraid that they were about to fall into each others' arms in warm embrace and shed rivers of tears on each other's shoulders, like in a melodrama.

"Wait a minute!" interjected the young jurist. "Let's be very clear here. I happen to be a rationalist. Mythology is not really my cup of tea. All right, fellows? Are you telling us, my dear captain, that the old patriarch is related to the minister? And that the minister wants to save this man because the two of them share the same blood, as your people like to say? Are you sure you don't take us for complete morons, my dear captain? All right then, I am a quadroon—one half black, a quarter white, two quarters . . ."

"Oh no, that can't be," said the captain, laughing for the first time. "That's already one quarter too many."

"Oh! So soldiers have a sense of humor now? Pronunciamentos are no longer your only specialty? Soldiers can evolve into human beings, can they? Is that possible? Well, my roots are all over the world, that is what I was trying to say, and I couldn't care less. So you don't actually think that I'm going to swallow all this, do you? A high-ranking guy, the second-most important man in the country, would compromise his career, would ultimately set all hell loose, would ignite the burning coals of civil discord up to and including bloody confrontation because he found out, God knows how, that some poor bastard . . . No, listen. And first of all, how did you find out?"

"How did we find out? That is a very good question, my dear counselor. Let me tell you then that this revelation reached us from the interior, as you like to call it in the opposition. Notables from several dozen clans spontaneously assembled when they learned of the situation. They dispatched a delegation of wise men knowledgeable in tradition and genealogy to us. These people can go back fifty generations from memory, my dear counselor, from memory alone."

"Blood lineage is sacred to us," the captain gravely continued, after vainly pausing to give the others a chance to jump in, "if you have not understood that, you have not understood anything about this country, Counselor. Ask your client. Go on and ask Narcisse. He is a rationalist too, although after his own fashion. Ask him."

The lawyer looked at Narcisse; the latter seemed suddenly ill at ease, like some miscreant forced to look subdued while being lectured by a traditionalist grandparent.

"Well, Narcisse, I'm listening."

"Well," Narcisse said, making coughing noises, "of course, I already knew the story the captain has just told us, although in a different version; but I didn't know that the agitation in our clans had reached such a pitch; all this can seem a bit strange to someone of our generation; yes, I realize that this might seem strange to you, but for our old folks, it is really very important. In fact, I think these stories may be what they really live for. It's true. . . ."

"So you believe it!" the young jurist insisted, shaking his head in disbelief.

"I didn't say that," Narcisse protested. "I didn't say that I actually believed it, but . . ."

"But what?" the lawyer asked. "Since when was consanguinity the mark of the most power-hungry adventurer in the entire history of mankind? It's idiotic, you have to admit. Do you think that if you stepped in his way, he would spare you because you share the same blood? Don't bet on it!"

"I didn't say that. I only said that it is very important to the old folks," Narcisse protested.

"Listen Narcisse, you are an educated man, an intellectual even; am I supposed to add devoutness to consanguinity among human rights?"

"I didn't say that," Narcisse replied, already irresistibly caught up in a euphoric and ethereal daydream at the thought that a blood relative might possibly run the country.

"You didn't say that, you didn't say that. . . ."

"No, I didn't say that," Narcisse continued. "All I said was . . ."

"So, my dear captain, what do we do now? This is all very well and good, but what does your minister without portfolio intend to do?"

The captain revealed to them that the situation was critical: the minister had made it clear to the chief of state that he could not allow the assassination of a man whose blood, in bespat-

The Story of the Madman

tering him, would tar his family with a sacrilege, thus damning it for all eternity. But that old imbecile remained obstinate and refused to see reason. So it had come to a showdown between the two men.

"It has gone that far?" Narcisse asked, torn between the dread of new confrontations between military factions and a vague sense of pride.

"After all, if those brutes are so keen to tear each other apart, they can go right ahead!" said the lawyer, rubbing his hands together, as soon as the captain had left them. "At least this is one cause no one can accuse me of losing; because I was going to lose it, there is no doubt about that; but given this new turn of events, the least that can be said is that the game is not over. Take my advice, my dear Narcisse, and get away from here as quickly as possible; there is trouble ahead. As for me, this kind of spectacle sends me into ecstasy. *Tu potes unanimos armare in proelia fratres atque odiis versare domos, tu verbera tectis funereasque inferre faces, tibi nomina mille, mille nocendi artes. . . .** A narrow-minded psychologist would probably accuse me of sadism. What can I say, that's the way I am."

Soon, insiders and their entourage glibly started to bet against each other on the imminence of a confrontation between the two camps. They speculated on the form it would take and how long it would last.

It was generally owned that the chief of state would certainly muster a larger quantity of arms and troops than his adversary but that, on the other hand, the minister had excellent strategists, the most skillful leaders of men, and especially the best positions, since the regiments that supported him were stationed in the barracks of the capital and its environs.

Even if, in the worst possible scenario, the minister's men allowed their adversaries to take the initiative, all they would need to do, once the fighting had begun, was to deploy throughout

---

*You can arm for combat brothers living in harmony, you can pour hatred into homes, you can carry whips and funeral torches inside; you have a thousand pretexts, a thousand ways of harming them (Virgil, *Aeneid* 7.336, West translation).
—*Translator's note*

the capital itself, where they could quickly neutralize the chief of state's partisans, occupy the various ministries, and take over the radio and television broadcasting station. A single day's worth of proclamations, falsely announcing the rallying of enemy troops or of prominent provincial figures to their side, would give them the appearance of legitimacy.

At the same time, they would dispatch elite troops to set up staggered barricades along the few roads linking the various provinces to the capital. Preventing the advance of hostile troops would then be an elementary strategic procedure. Within a hundred-kilometer radius around the capital, the landscape was made up of moderately to highly dense forests, where it would be difficult for one side to advance and easy for the other to hide from the likely air raids.

After which, the only thing remaining for the minister's men to do would be to have the deposed president tried by a military tribunal, which would condemn him to die; that was now the customary way of proceeding. It had become something of a cultural tradition.

But, others would argue, a skillful use of assets by the chief of state could not fail to scuttle his adversary's maneuver. After all, could not the faction of the army that supported him, being larger, easily cut off the capital, buried as it was in the interior of the country, block its supply lines, and, in effect, slowly asphyxiate it?

For it is an established fact, if we are to believe the united chorus of polemical theoreticians, that time unfailingly favors the greater number, as demonstrated by the various campaigns undertaken by the greatest conquerors Europe ever produced to subjugate Russia, which have all invariably ended in the defeat of genius against the wall of the multitude.

To clinch the matter one had only to consider that, besides this numerical advantage, the military supporters of the chief of state were also better armed. Airplanes and helicopters had the specific capacity of pulverizing and setting ablaze obstacles such as barrages and all sorts of minor forts. By sowing the kind of terror that bombing raids and massive destruction inspire, they could break the staunchest determinations, sow doubt everywhere, freeze enthusiasm, and set off routs, the usual prelude to retreat.

"Once in the capital," concluded the lawyer, who was a virtuoso of inspired tirades, "the personal guards of the chief of state would be able to quickly neutralize the minister's partisans, occupy the various ministries, and take over the radio and television broadcasting station. A single day's worth of proclamations, falsely announcing the rallying of enemy troops or of prominent provincial figures to their side, would give them the appearance of legitimacy. After which, the only thing remaining for the chief of state's men to do would be to have the vanquished minister tried by a military tribunal, which would condemn him to die; that was now the customary way of proceeding. It has become something of a cultural tradition—or a bit of folklore, if you prefer. *Ardet inexcita Ausonia atque immobilis ante.*"*

However, there were certain parameters that could not be ignored and which rendered all prognostications particularly uncertain. How, for example, would the civilian population react, and would they weigh in significantly enough to offset the scourge of a stalemate?

The capital and its surroundings were indubitably the minister's constituency, since the inhabitants belonged to the ethnic group to which this high-level dignitary had always claimed, with apparent reason, to belong—abusing, like a true demagogue, this advantage. In addition, the eastern portion of the country, inhabited by populations that shared numerous cultural traditions with the ethnic group residing in the capital and its surroundings, was admittedly not hostile to him.

On the other hand, in the unanimous opinion of the clandestine press and of the insiders and their entourage, the ethnic group residing in the North, which had been transformed by its religion and social organization into a force to be reckoned with, bore the chief of state an affection bordering on devotion. Like a true demagogue, he too abused this advantage. The rest

---

*Ausonia, unaroused and quiet until that moment, is aflame (Virgil, *Aeneid* 7.623, West translation). —*Translator's note*

of the country, where most of the population lived, displayed neither like nor dislike for the two protagonists in this war of giants whose dark clouds increasingly darkened the horizon with the promise of an apocalyptic storm.

Moreover, the stance and ulterior motives of the former colonial power gave rise to conjectures as extravagant as they were contradictory. Alternating between a debonair savoir faire, underhandedness, and cynicism, this western power, bolstered by its honorability and especially by its skillfully maintained image of generosity and modernity, had pulled off the gambit of keeping some African republics, whose legal status amounted theoretically to full sovereignty, in the humiliating position of colonial protectorates.

Its military interventions on the African continent were countless; in fact, they were now so much a part of normal international diplomacy that they no longer raised any criticism. The powerless African elite and leaders had to take its iron rule into account the same way they did the changing of the seasons, seismic tremors, or any other so-called natural cataclysms.

Some believed that the chief of state was the darling of the former colonial power and that it would never, under any circumstances, abandon him. It would send its soldiers if the dictator were in any way threatened. Others held that it was surreptitiously encouraging the minister, who had promised to give it complete control over the exploitation of national oil if he became the master. It would, therefore, ostensibly abstain from intervening, as long as the minister's victory was prompt and problem-free.

An optimistic faction, branded as utopians, speculated on what they perceived to be a certain weariness on the part of this guardian after thirty years of supporting dictators. It was no doubt secretly hoping to promote the dawn of democratic regimes and henceforth would place what had customarily been called its aid in the service of this evolution, although that term was considered wholly inadequate in university circles, traditionally hostile to its tutelage.

Another current of thought, dominated by the lawyer, claimed exclusive lucidity and the strictest rationalism, professing that the politics of the guardian power was nothing other than the application of realpolitik; the explanation for the changes about to occur in the leadership of African nations derived from the fears inspired by the next session of the General Assembly of the United Nations; the question of the former colonial power's last colonies in America and in Oceania as well as, generally speaking, its rank in the concert of nations —overrated at this point according to some—would be discussed. It was rumored that Japan, now essentially the second great power in the world and second only to the United States of America as the financial backer of international institutions, was eyeing with increasing impatience one of the five permanent seats on the Security Council, two of which were occupied, admittedly undeservedly although no one said so openly, by a pair of somewhat wheezy, not to say decrepit, western nations. And the guardian power was cast into the throes of despair at the mere thought of being forced to surrender the proud trophy that masked its decline. In order to exorcise the horrible nightmare of a mortifying headlong plunge into the pit of anonymous peoples, was it not of the utmost importance, henceforth, to rally a majority of allied or obligated nations and escape the dreaded verdict of the organization in this humiliating juncture?

There were even some people, who admittedly were dismissed as jokers or corrupt individuals and consequently considered faithless and lawless, who claimed that the former colonial power was in no way responsible for the convulsions of the republic, these being nothing more, according to them, than the manifestations of Africans' incapacity to govern themselves as a modern nation.

The breathless anticipation of battle gradually became a desire to see it happen, as if it would bring the answers to all the public's questions.

One night, it appeared as if it had started, because, in the usually badly lit capital, the sections of the city where luxury shops were located were suddenly illuminated by a blinding light, while rapid crackling noises, which could have been exploding bombs or grenades, sounded sporadically seemingly all across town. The sirens of fire trucks gave way to the interminable telltale wails of ambulances.

But dawn broke on a city where the scenes of daily routine unfolded in their usual monotonous fashion. It had been a false alert. The crestfallen residents dejectedly went off to their offices, workshops, and street stalls.

Yet there was one man in the capital who, far from losing his composure, confidently paced the luxurious quarters of his marble palace awaiting the sinister miracle he had been promised: it was the chief of state. The events that followed would cause him the most acute disappointment ever suffered by a tyrant.

ALTHOUGH IT WAS then under the iron rule of the inflexible Zoaétoa, the tribe shows unanimous agreement on only one point: it was indeed very early in the morning that, after two days and three nights of labor, the little fiancée was shaken by the spasms that preceded the expulsion of the fetus. As for the rest, there are as many versions of the phenomenon as there are adult residents.

After a long investigation, I managed to come up with the following synthesis, short of the authentic version that no one seemed able to reconstruct owing to how intensely disturbed the populace was over this unprecedented event in the annals of the province, maybe even of the republic.

Initially, the child appeared to be stillborn, neither crying nor moving, all wrinkled up, and looking like a cross between a cynocephalus baby and a tadpole. No doubt about it, the little fiancée had given birth to a monster. The traditional circle of midwives shuddered in revulsion and collectively shrunk back.

Yet soon afterward a sort of shiver ran through the strange creature who now looked part lower mammal, part reptile, and part saurian; he appeared to be faintly and anarchically stretching his limbs with the imperceptible undulations of an agonizing snake. Then, the more patient observers thought they saw the creature convulsively opening its mouth, or what served as such, and emitting, at very long intervals, barely perceptible rattles.

A whole hour, possibly even two, went by after the expulsion of the fetus before the despairing midwives regained their faith.

The Story of the Madman

"It is a human being, a viable child!" the senior midwife exclaimed, swooping in to take the newborn into her peasant's palm. "Look at that, look at him! I could hold two like him in my hand; did I say two, make that three or four. . . ."

The senior midwife did not know how right she was. The young mother continued to be shaken by spasms, and a second male child arrived. Around noon there were three. But the spasms continued. Alerted by drum calls, processions of skeptics converged from everywhere, swelling the dense crowd that had assembled outside like believers adoring a hidden idol.

A fourth male child was born at around three o'clock in the afternoon, and the crowd was seized by a paroxysm of mixed astonishment, panic, and jubilation. When the fifth boy arrived as night was falling, the crowd ran away convinced that thunder was about to strike the roof that sheltered the accursed mother.

When the night was over, the crowds returned. Panic had given way to a religious daze.

Surprisingly, when the two women doctors attached to the office of the minister of health learned of this almost unbelievable event, they jumped into a trailer without asking their employer for permission, despite the fact that they had always, until then, trembled at the mere mention of his name. Gripped by an odd feeling of pity, not unrelated to remorse, they hastened to the side of the young mother and of her monstrous brood. At their bedside, they unpacked a pile of objects that had never been seen before in Zoaételeu's village. The sight of plastic bottles nauseated as well as mystified the traditional circle of midwives.

"We do this for a living," the women doctors explained to the stunned midwives. "It is imperative that you trust us and allow us a free hand, otherwise you will be responsible for these children's doom. Quintuplets are extremely fragile newborns; look at them, they are barely bigger than chicks. They will die one after the other unless they receive intensive, round-the-clock care."

And, under the watchful eyes of the midwives, they bustled around these small chicks of indeterminate species who, thanks to these women whom remorse had suddenly transformed, were on that day miraculously saved from the first aggressions of life, against all the lessons of experience and the doctrines of established beliefs.

The minister of health, an *agrégé* in medicine, arrived unexpectedly; he had been informed of the two women doctors' escapade and had interrogated his underlings until he had learned the reason.

The two women thought he would heap reproaches on them; they prepared to respond with the sarcastic bitterness and rebelliousness that tyrannical superiors deserve. They had preemptively secured the support of the new master of the community, Zoaétoa, by sketching an odious portrait of the powerful man. Zoaétoa, who was more inflexible than the Fate Atropos, as Narcisse's lawyer friend would later say, had just declared war on a government that persisted in victimizing his venerable father. To the women doctors' astonishment, the minister of health, an *agrégé* in medicine, congratulated them and even offered them encouragement. There was no rhyme or reason to it.

The old missionary from the neighboring evangelical establishment also voiced his sympathy and support to the women doctors, whose devotion he commended; he did not forget to hail, in a wide gesture of benediction, the entrance of the five chicks into the world, this vale of tears. He paid no attention to their mother, possibly because, having conceived outside the sacred bonds of Christian marriage, she was supposed to be in a state of sin.

The lawyer arrived as well, dragging behind him a more embarrassed than delighted Narcisse. He was nothing like other fathers; he was a father who seemed to want to hide in the bowels of the earth instead of rejoicing by jumping up and down as any other father in creation would have done under these exhilarating circumstances.

"Narcisse, this is a glorious day for you. Go on and kiss this admirable mother, as a gratified father should. Take her in your arms and embrace her as if you would make your two bodies one forever. That is how a father conscious of his duty should treat her," the lawyer whispered to him repeatedly before the young man, taking his courage in both hands, finally resigned himself to obeying him.

Eventually, Narcisse reluctantly complied, while the whole family, as if on cue, broke into a storm of shouts, of applause, of songs, and of chants, for it is traditional to congratulate happy fathers noisily. And Narcisse should have been five times happier than an ordinary father.

"You see," the lawyer said to him, congratulating him in his own fashion, "you see what ecstasy you would have deprived your family of! Bravo, my friend, bravo twice over. You are a great man, but you didn't know it. Now you know."

Government journalists bearing video recorders, cameras, or simply pens soon made their intrusion upon the scene. They all seemed to be brimming over with love, gushing out promises of reconciliation, and displaying the most heartfelt admiration. They professed themselves outraged at the frigid reserve displayed by Zoaétoa, the new master of the community, as well as by the sarcasm of the lawyer, who remained true to form.

"What are you doing here?" he asked them, perched on an improvised stage and speaking in Zoaétoa's name. "Who invited you? What do you have in common with these poor people? Are you not ashamed to show your faces here when you have done nothing but disparage the august sage of this community? You remind me of Caesar presiding over the funeral of his victim, Pompey, who had been foully subjected to mutilation. You are vile vultures, emulators of Scylla, who devoured with her eyes, short of being able to do so with her teeth, the severed heads of her enemies whom she had condemned to die under the most painful torture. Go away, get out of here, you carrion-scavenging hyenas masquerading as scribes."

The lawyer, who was an accomplished actor, was aware that in this country no attempt to impress fools could possibly be excessive. So, as he spoke, he shook his fist, threw back his head, rolled his eyes around like two lotto balls, and swayed from one side to the other. Under this remonstration, the government journalists resheathed their instruments, but, far from leaving the area as they were being asked to do, they cunningly remained on the sidelines like cringing dogs, convinced that such

The Story of the Madman

an unusual set of circumstances could not unfold without providing them with some fodder. Their sordid hopes were about to be fulfilled.

In the meantime, the world seemed to have suddenly been transformed on that magical day. The puny had grown big and the bad had turned good; the unknown shone with brilliance and those who were remote moved closer. The great leaned down and the most closed of faces smiled. Egoists strove for generosity. Clouds melted at the approach of the sun.

The epidemic of joy reached even the colonel commanding the garrison in the neighboring town. He arrived in the village that he had once mortified with his haughtiness and insensitivity, surrounded, like the great chief he was, by the richly bedecked characters of his entire staff with their jutting necks, not to mention their prowling fox miens, their scowling faces, and their menacing glares. He was preceded by two troop carriers crammed with soldiers and followed at a distance by four light armored cars and three self-propelled rocket launchers. The soldiers, in combat uniform, sprang out from under the tarpaulins as if for action and quickly formed a corridor for the great chief and his entire staff to enter the village. The colonel commanding the garrison expressed the desire to see the quintuplets, who, as he pompously stated, were an unprecedented phenomenon that would soon echo around the world.

Prompted by Zoaétoa and by the two women doctors, who were now irrevocably converted to a rebellious frame of mind, the traditional circle of midwives, like a coop of mother hens opening their wings to ward off an attack, declared his request null and void and formed a barrier against the colonel and his entire staff. That confirmed bully, to whose will everyone had always before bent, found it inconceivable that anyone could be so bold as to reject one of his requests, especially one expressed in a tone of command. The colonel was about to force his way in when Zoaétoa mobilized the tribe, its ranks swollen by countless sympathizers, for the second assault in its long history against established authority.

The representatives of the state found themselves instantly caught in a vice of young combatants whose eyes shone with bellicose fire. The soldiers instinctively reached for their belts as if to draw their weapons. The vice tightened around them. Were guns about to do the talking?

For the first time in his life, the lawyer intervened to nip civil discord in the bud instead of being content to observe a spectacle that promised to plunge him into ecstasy.

"Colonel," he boomed effectively, "could you be so base as to open fire on unarmed peasants? Put away your weapon and order your men to do the same. I, in turn, pledge to convince these good people to allow you to leave with your honor intact and without physically assaulting you."

And that is what happened, especially after Narcisse, speaking in the name of the unfortunate patriarch and as the representative of all thirty-two ancestral generations, had also enjoined the soldiers in a noble and grave manner to leave the premises. He had finally consented to brave the dangers of public action and even to expose himself to violence. No one was more surprised than himself that he came out of the encounter unscathed. It was truly a glorious day for him, and for the Latin-speaking lawyer, it was another chance to humiliate the military and to make more enemies within its ranks.

Turning toward the pack of government journalists gathered together to the side, the lawyer shook his fist at them.

"I hope you are satisfied now, you bunch of cowering scribes? Your patience has been rewarded. Go on, don't be finicky, you have gotten your fodder. Don't tell us that you are not satiated. We can already guess what filth you are going to propagate. A phenomenal event that should have led to a day of festivity and of unity has once more provided a pretext to the village of the accursed marabout to defy the legitimate government of the republic. Isn't that your style?"

Upon which, the government pen pushers lowered their heads, turned on their heels, and, one after the other, disappeared into their spanking new limousines and left.

Thus, Narcisse's day of glory ended in an entirely unexpected way. The same could not be said of what followed. From that point on, events would unfold according to a relentless logic.

Initially, the chief of state summoned his close advisors, the next-to-last most intimate circle of the faithful. They had each been lectured that very day by their respective official mentors in various foreign embassies, but the chief of state did not know it.

"Gentlemen, this is the moment of truth. Let me have your opinions," he demanded.

The spokesman for the close advisors replied courageously on this occasion.

"Your Excellency," he said, "as you know, public opinion has taken over this painful business. The old fetishist has the upper hand more than ever. He is no longer the instigator of a criminal conspiracy but a patriarch protected by Providence itself. . . . How can such a man be sent to a firing squad without setting off popular rebellion, not to mention eventual international condemnation, which is as inevitable as it would be disastrous in our situation? But there is worse. How can such a man be sentenced to death without inviting the wrath of the spirits who are silently observing us and without exposing ourselves to their curse? Consider what sacrilege would forever mar our lives, Your Excellency. It is time we earned the benevolence of the ancestors, who have just indicated to us, with the unprecedented birth of five children, all male, all from the same mother, all on the same day, and all viable, the person on whom Destiny has bestowed its favor in this instance. Your Excellency, free this fortunate old man, blessed by the otherworld, and appease the spirits of the ancestors."

The chief of state appeared to have suddenly aged by a few

decades. He was dejected and silent; his head was bowed. He nervously and uncharacteristically puffed on an enormous cigar. How changed he was!

"Quintuplets," he finally said, despondently, "quintuplets! Is the old sorcerer really the father? That's an important point."

"There are different versions circulating on the subject," the spokesman for the close advisors answered. "Some say that he is in fact the father. According to the clandestine newspapers, Narcisse is the father."

"Narcisse? Who is this Narcisse?" the chief of state inquired, with his head still bowed and nervously drawing on his enormous cigar.

"He is one of the old sorcerer's sons; he testified at the trial."

"What is the truth, in your opinion?" the chief of state asked in a discouraged voice. "Who is the real father? The sorcerer? His son? This is crucial. Who can tell me?"

The close advisors were divided on this point.

"What? You don't know?" the chief of state flared. "Are you not paid to know these things? What have I done to the good Lord? Why can't I have real advisors? Didn't I pay you enough? All the other chiefs of state have real advisors. . . . But me, I ruin myself and what do I get? Losers! That's what you are, all of you, losers! Losers! Losers! . . ."

And the chief of state made a show of lapsing into bitter weeping. But was he really only pretending?

"What does it matter," the spokesman for the intimate advisors courageously interjected, with a tinge of annoyance. "What does it matter, Your Excellency, whether it is the son or the father? Providence has clearly spoken, that is the essential point. It is undeniable that that family has been blessed by the ancestors and by the lord of the otherworld."

Not completely convinced but now riddled with doubts, the chief of state then summoned his family council, the most intimate circle of the faithful, the ramparts of his pride and of his equanimity. Its members remained shrouded in silence with the exception of the minister of health, an *agrégé* in medicine, and of the specialist in applied psychology, who fraudulently claimed to be a doctoral candidate in that field from the University of Rouen.

According to the latter, the present juncture was marked by panic and hysteria, the two breasts that traditionally nurture the abdication of legitimate governments.

"Under such circumstances," he declared sententiously, "all the great experts of my discipline recommend composure and even a phlegmatic attitude. To remain phlegmatic in stormy situations is the key to success and to the longevity of legitimate governments."

"Let us be realistic," retorted the minister of health, an *agrégé* in medicine. "The public is convinced that, through these extraordinary births, Providence has indicated its favor toward our adversary, who is now praised by everyone. What can we do? If we persist, we will alienate the interior."

"For how long?" the chief of state asked.

"It's impossible to say," answered the minister of health, *agrégé* in medicine.

"Public opinion, public opinion. We create public opinion," the specialist in applied psychology declared. "The stronger and more resolute we appear, the more inclined the public will be to revere us and to accept our views and our decisions. Public opinion is the alibi of surrender and cowardice. There is no such thing as public opinion, there is only the authority of radiant certainty. Let us not allow ourselves to be stripped of our authority. Let us not appear to doubt ourselves. Let us be strong, and everyone will believe that we are strong. Caress the rabble and it will bite you; strike it and it will lick your hand. It works the same way as with a dog."

Although they were repeatedly questioned, the other members of the family council remained obstinately silent, devoured now by the uncertainty of tomorrows that promised to be stormy; they found themselves facing a reversal they would never have imagined possible.

The chief of state left, ungraciously abandoning his relatives in an oppressive state of confusion. It was only when he slept with an unknown woman that night, as he did every night, that he reached his decision. He found his ephemeral partner strangely tense and cold, in other words, unsuitable for the act of love. This vexed the chief of state so much that he interrupted his passion. The young woman started to cry, and the chief of state wanted to know why.

"Your Excellency," she said, "I beg you, don't hold it against me; you are our father, our God, I want to please you, but I'm so afraid."

Intrigued and moved, the chief of state asked, "What are you afraid of, my child?"

"What? Don't you know what is being said all over town?" she asked.

"What is that, my girl?"

"I'm afraid to tell you, Your Excellency. Promise that you won't be angry with me if I tell you; I was sure that you already knew. Everyone is saying it, no one who has ears can help hearing it."

"What is being said? Come on, tell me! That's an order."

"Your Excellency," the girl said painfully, after a long hesitation, "it is rumored that your fate is sealed and that the fatal outcome will not be long now. They say that Providence has made it abundantly clear by bestowing five male children, born of the same mother, from the same pregnancy, and on the same day to the sorcerer. They say that such a thing is unheard of and that this phenomenon can only be a verdict from the otherworld. They say that those who come near you will suffer the same deplorable fate. I am so frightened, Your Excellency," the girl added through chattering teeth. "I am petrified; that is why I was not able to please you."

"You have nothing to worry about," the chief of state answered. "Don't be afraid, my child. I am here, look at me, I will protect you. Nothing can happen to you while you are with me. I am strong, I am the chief; everyone obeys me, everyone bows before me."

Since the girl had stopped crying, the chief of state attempted a new assault, which was as unsuccessful as the first.

It was an atrocious night, during which the chief of state was

The Story of the Madman

unable to get any sleep. The next day, he thought he discerned that members of his family edged away from him or avoided crossing his path. His close relatives, including his own children, whose insatiable greed he knew well, did not come around to solicit passes, or recommendations for the banks, or free rides on the national airline. The volume of his appointments plummeted. The mothers of the privileged families that made up the so-called high society neglected coming to depict for him, with artful enumeration, the charms of their barely pubescent daughters. His horoscope proved ambiguous and somewhat on the gloomy side. He decided to consult his own sorcerer, but only as a formality, for he had already settled on a course of action since the revelations of his ephemeral companion.

"Your Excellency," the man with the evasive glance courageously told him, "it is all going badly, it is all intangible. Times have never been so uncertain. You must reconcile yourself with the occult forces now."

"But how?" the chief of state asked.

"Free that man!" the sorcerer exhorted him. "He is obstructing your destiny; he is like a boulder blocking the bed where the river of your power flows. Free that man, I tell you."

"Man? What man?" the chief of state asked, pretending not to understand.

"The man who is blessed by the gods. Free the sorcerer, Zoaételeu, whom Providence has just honored with five male children from one pregnancy, from the same mother, and on the same day. It is a phenomenon that has never been seen before, Your Excellency. There can be no other explanation than this: this man enjoys the favor of occult forces. Free him to stave off misfortune."

"And if I refuse?" the chief of state asked.

"Then I see horror everywhere, a frightful sequence of events, dark pools of blood spilled on glaucous asphalt, dismembered corpses, shattered skulls. In short, I cannot answer for the consequences, Your Excellency."

"But that old man is not the father," the chief of state protested. "His son is. That has been established."

"What does it matter, Your Excellency," the sorcerer answered. "A father or his son, it is all the same. Free the magician who is blessed by the gods."

At six o'clock in the evening of the same day, the chief of state sent the order to the prosecutor of the military tribunal to release Zoaételeu.

No sooner said than done, for the wishes of the chief of state had the particularity of brooking no arguments or delays.

The release order, which was meant to be secret like all the other major decisions of that government, was, according to another rarely belied custom, uncovered by rogue government employees, who leaked it to the lawyer's supporters. They in turn informed journalists from the clandestine press, which was increasingly less so. Plans were made to organize a triumphant escort to accompany the patriarch back to his village, some hundred kilometers away.

This plan was in turn uncovered by the chief of the gendarmerie, the son of the first cousin of the chief of state and the supreme master of public order in the capital. The only remedy he came up with to counter the popular plot, was to discreetly kidnap the old man and transport him back to his village by helicopter, with no consideration for what possible consequences such a late initiation to flying might have on an old man already exhausted by weeks of imprisonment. But it was evidently written that Zoaételeu would survive everything.

When he arrived, everything that the colonel commanding the neighboring garrison had previously seized had been returned to him, including the television set and the generator. Thus, surrounded by his tribe, including Narcisse's little fiancée, who, in her role as miracle mother, was now revered as an idol, and his quintuplet grandchildren, jealously cared for by their benevolent nannies, the patriarch was able to vicariously live the events occurring in the capital and of which he was, unwittingly and initially unknowingly, the hero.

Crowds flooded the screen like the rising tide of a river swollen by the rains, now calm and motionless, now stormy. Here and there, some posters could be seen on which, the educated villagers told the patriarch, his name was written in giant letters.

The Story of the Madman

"But why?" he asked them.

"They are celebrating your release," Zoaétoa explained to him. "It is a great day because you are a great man now. Right now, you are probably the greatest man in the whole country. Look at that poster, yes the highest one, the one a gloved hand is holding up. It reads: *Zoaételeu has moved the mountain, for Zoaételeu has lifted the first stone. Long live Zoaételeu.*"

"Is that a saying?" the patriarch asked. "And what does it mean? How did I move the mountain? And first of all, what mountain?"

No one was able to tell him the meaning of the enigmatic dithyramb.

The eloquent and well-dressed young man who had been his lawyer suddenly appeared in the foreground; his lips were moving and he held his arms high over his head; he was waving them about. He perched himself on the roof of a car, signaled to the crowd, and pointed with his finger. The crowd then opened to make way for another young man, who was immediately hoisted up next to the lawyer, joining him on the roof of the car. The newcomer was at first nonplused and awkward, like a frightened man, then he began to gesticulate in time with the lawyer; he too raised his arms over his head, moved his lips feverishly, and took on a dramatic expression.

"Why, that's Narcisse!" the old man exclaimed. "That's my son!"

As if they had only been waiting for the patriarch's outburst, jets of water suddenly erupted from all around, flooding and disbanding the crowd, and knocking the lawyer and Narcisse head over heels as the screen suddenly went blank.

Without any directives, without consulting with each other, the tribe remained frozen around the screen. But time passed and the screen remained blank; alarming whispers then began to circulate around the assembly to the effect that Narcisse had no doubt been killed. The perennial patrol of uniformed men happened to be passing by; the villagers stopped them to find out what they could.

The men in uniform had become more human since the patriarch's return; they now condescended to converse with the

The Story of the Madman

villagers, showing them a sort of friendliness and even a measure of consideration. Nevertheless, sometimes their eyes shone with a curious light, like the one that can be seen in a leopard's eyes when, perchance, blinded by the intoxication of the hunt, that pitiless animal enters a clearing where a carelessly extinguished fire still smolders. They said that they were not better informed than the villagers; the radio in their jeep had also gone dead, probably at the same time as the television screen.

They agreed to stop in the village and share in the joy of the villagers, whose patriarch had just been returned to them.

"It might be a putsch," they finally admitted, as the villagers continued to press them with questions.

"What is a putsch?" the villagers asked.

"When a great chief is not happy with his wages, he gathers his faithful supporters and storms the presidential palace," they answered, chortling with laughter. "If everything goes well, he captures the chief of state, throws him in jail, and takes his place and his wages. It's normal, it's logical. That is what a putsch is."

"It's nothing but a matter of wages?" the peasants asked in wonder. "But then, why do people die?"

"It's simple," the young men continued, still chortling with laughter. "You have to understand. Soldiers have weapons. That's why people die. Otherwise, what would be the use of having weapons? Do you understand? When you have weapons, of course you use them, and people die. And a soldier has to have weapons; if he didn't, he wouldn't be a soldier, do you see?"

That was apparently too subtle a dialectic for the peasants; or it may be that the uniformed men, hailing from a province neighboring the one native to the chief, spoke the villagers' language very badly; the latter obsessively harked back to the same question:

"But if it's only a question of wages, why do people have to die?"

"You must be worrying about your Narcisse," the soldiers concluded. "We are going back to the garrison, and tomorrow morning, you'll know how things stand. Don't worry, nothing has happened to him."

The Story of the Madman

Just then, children's shouts alerted everyone to the fact that the television was on again. They all rushed in.

Zoaételeu and his family, convinced that Narcisse would be swallowed up by the storm, lived every hour of the putsch that toppled the chief of state and his large family like an agony.

A richly bedecked character, resembling the late colonel the first time he came to the village, was seen unfolding a sheet of paper and sternly reading a long proclamation. This was unquestionably a dramatic occurrence. The patriarch consulted the ten members of his educated sector. Opinions were split. According to some, war had just been declared against a foreign nation; others claimed that if there was in fact a war, it must be between the chief of state and his large family on the one hand and their adversaries gathered around the minister without portfolio on the other—the dissension between them having long ceased to be a secret even for the lowliest among the population.

Columns of tanks and troop carriers raced across city squares. Helmeted soldiers ran, ducking behind walls every now and then; they quickly scaled obstacles; they set their machine guns and mortars into position and opened fire, their hands vibrating on the gleaming steel. A raging fire engulfed the floors of an imposing building. Panicked civilians fled beneath swirling spirals of sinister black smoke, shielding their heads with their hands. Airplanes and other machines, which the patriarch's educated sector could now name and which were, in fact, helicopters, took turns streaking across the sky, every so often dropping bombs that, upon striking public buildings or homes, produced horrible explosions drowned out by the military music playing in the background.

Pinned to the ground, a child opened a grimacing mouth, probably to let out a howl of pain and despair, as his hand clawed at his bleeding leg.

Next came a cluster of decorated military men standing in front of a map, conferring with each other and shaking their heads convulsively. Then, an official in a suit and tie repeatedly raised his arms to the sky in what was surely a sign of triumph.

The screen went dark and, after a long wait, lit up once more.

The richly bedecked character reappeared; he was smiling. He made a statement that the educated villagers did not all understand in the same way, but the images that followed left little doubt that the chief of state and his large family had been routed. Their now vanquished government was displayed to the viewers. In the center of the group stood the frivolous prosecutor, at whose appearance the usually peace-loving Zoaételeu burst out in a vengeful cry; the young officer, once so dashing, detached, and arrogant, held his head bowed and was disheveled, barefoot, and unshaven in his civilian clothes. A helmeted soldier walked up to him and struck him on the temple with the butt of his gun; a grimace clenched the face of the commander, formerly the frivolous prosecutor, and he collapsed.

Then the screen showed a column of soldiers in fatigues, bareheaded, barefoot, disheveled also, heads bowed, and as unkempt as the commander, formerly the frivolous prosecutor. On an order issued by a drill officer, they squatted with their hands crossed over their heads, then, in one motion, lay face down on the asphalt. For a whole week, the screen was filled with more such images.

Neither Narcisse nor the lawyer had been swallowed by the storm. The two men resurfaced in the village, arm in arm like two merry companions, the day after the upheaval and related the entire affair to the patriarch, as he sat surrounded by his daughter-in-law and by the quintuplets like so many fetishes.

The men of the minister without portfolio had not left any initiatives open to their opponents, who had been essentially trapped in the middle of crowds that were protesting against tyranny for the first time since independence. All they had needed to do was to deploy throughout the capital itself, where they had been able to quickly neutralize the chief of state's partisans, occupy the various ministries, and take over the radio and television broadcasting station. A single day's worth of proclamations falsely announcing the rallying of enemy troops or of prominent provincial figures to their side had given them the appearance of legitimacy. At the same time, they had sent out elite troops who had set up staggered barricades along the

The Story of the Madman

few roads linking the various provinces to the capital. Preventing the advance of hostile troops had then been an elementary strategic procedure. Within a hundred-kilometer radius around the capital, the landscape was made up of moderately to highly dense forests, where it had been difficult for the one side to advance and easy for the other to hide from air raids.

After which, the only thing remaining for the minister's men to do was to have the deposed chief of state tried by a military tribunal, which, predictably, had condemned him to die; that was now the customary way of proceeding.

"The new great chief gave a speech yesterday," the patriarch said to Narcisse. "I heard him, I happened to be in front of the television set right then. He was speaking our language. Is he one of us?"

"Yes, Father," Narcisse replied, a note of enthusiasm in his voice. "He is one of us, can you imagine?"

"One of you, one of you," snapped the lawyer, whose roots were all over the globe, who spoke several languages and understood even more. "What do these military asses care about being one of you? Soldiers have no ethnicity, no religion, they recognize neither father nor mother, they don't believe in anything for this very simple reason: they have no brain. No brain, therefore no soul."

"But he is still one of us," insisted Narcisse, who was unrecognizable, his eyes lit up by an animal passion.

"Stop talking nonsense," the lawyer retorted. "Not to mention that, just wait . . . it's not over, old buddy. A faction of the army remains faithful to the former chief of state. Now, let's assume that his successor, God forbid, decides to do him in. What would happen? The capital, which is enclosed, don't forget, would be besieged and probably asphyxiated by troops that, short of any evidence to the contrary, are superior in number and better armed. The planes and helicopters of the former chief of state have yet to enter the fray. Take my word for it, this is still playing itself out. I only hope that the new guy isn't foolish enough to have his predecessor assassinated. But what else can you expect from a soldier?"

The Story of the Madman

"Even so," Narcisse opined, "for once that it is one of our own, you can let us strut a little can't you, even if it doesn't really mean anything? It is still the first time that one of us has moved into the palace."

"You haven't heard the last of this, man," the disgusted lawyer finally replied. "What do you bet that we haven't heard the last of it?"

B<small>Y DINT OF</small> much skill and perseverance, the captain managed to find Narcisse.

"How wonderful to finally see you again, my brother, now that we are the masters of the country! Did you see how we demolished them? It was great. They didn't see it coming, right? What do you think? So, what are you up to these days? What are your plans? Do you want to join us? We have a place ready for you. . . ."

Narcisse was offered, pell-mell, a position as embassy secretary, a job as subprefect, an appointment as police inspector following a training course in Europe, the stewardship of a lycée as headmaster, a post of deputy in a ministry or in a state enterprise. . . . The hard part would be which to choose.

"Those or something else," the captain added. "All you have to do is ask, and your wishes will be granted immediately. And do you know who sent me? Your buddy Osomnanga. You may laugh, but he is partially responsible for the appointments. He is the president's favorite advisor."

Narcisse, who had learned how to get rich through fraudulent import with exemption from custom duties, did not wish to change professions. Being little inclined to the pleasures of vanity, he more than ever felt most at home in the shadows behind the scenes. He promised to think it over and to give his answer later. Several other meetings between the two men ended the same way.

"Why don't you make these offers to Zoaétoa, my elder brother?" Narcisse stubbornly repeated to the captain. "He's the one you should be talking to. He is the man for the job."

The captain was an obstinate man. He was also no doubt being pressured by the new chief of state, formerly the minister without portfolio, who longed to establish his reign on Zoaételeu the patriarch and his descendants. The captain confided his unsuccessful efforts to Osomnanga, who took him to Zoaételeu's village. When the villagers recognized Osomnanga, they showed him a veneration almost equal to that enjoyed by the patriarch himself.

Zoaétoa, in his role as regent, and with the villagers following suit, pointed at the chief of state's advisor and told the old man, "Here's the man who saved you! Without him you would have been shot."

Osomnanga and the patriarch fell into each other's arms. They did indeed share the same blood. In the joy of their reunion, which lasted into the evening, they continuously went from tears to shouts of laughter, from the merriest laughter to the most bitter tears.

"Speak, my son, speak," the old man said to Osomnanga, "do not hesitate. Ask and I will give you everything I have. I have very little, but you only have to say the word and I will give you everything. Do not hesitate, my son, speak. Look at all the pubescent adolescent girls around me. How many do you want? Ten? Fifteen?"

As for Osomnanga, speaking in the name of the new chief of state, he promised to gratify all the wishes of his venerable host, without whom the recent miracles would not have occurred. What did he wish for? A palace? It would be built. A car? Nothing easier. The chief of state wanted only one thing in return, the friendship of the patriarch and of his family, starting with Narcisse.

Was this only the dawn of Zoaételeu's happiness? A few days after Osomnanga's visit, the recently appointed colonel commanding the neighboring garrison arrived in the village surrounded by his entire staff. He was a field commander, like those who could now be seen every day on television, in his belted fatigues, his chest overflowing with decorations, his belly bulging, and his features frozen in the dumbfounded, blissful ex-

The Story of the Madman

pression common to those whom Providence has only recently favored. His staff, in his image, advanced nonchalantly, completely in tune with the climate of indolence in which the village had always basked. He was followed by a company that honored the patriarch, who was sitting in front of his house, with a military salute to the sound of martial music performed by a regimental band.

The visitors asked to see the quintuplets and the miraculous woman who had brought them into the world. The villagers were delighted to hear them speak their language fluently and recognized them as native sons.

The high point of fraternization occurred when the young captain, who accompanied the colonel although he was not part of his regiment, shed his fatigues and started to dance in front of the inhabitants, bare-chested, a loincloth tied around his waist, to the sound of the tom-toms. Initially dumbfounded, the villagers' explosion of joy inevitably escalated into delirium when they recognized in his entrechats, and in the twists of his hips and of his spine, the familiar steps of their culture.

And that is how, although Narcisse was careful to stay away from this party, Zoaételeu's village became a fiefdom of the new chief of state, formerly the minister without portfolio.

Finally, the new chief of state himself honored Zoaételeu with a visit. He was preceded by two elite companies, dispatched by the neighboring garrison town to prepare the populace for the event. The troops had to clear several hectares around the village to set up tents; they did some terracing to create and set up small avenues of communication; they dug wells to store water reserves. The peasants were too deeply overjoyed by the glorious status conferred on their community to wonder at how the ancestral site, unfenced and shorn of its traditional setting, had collapsed and disintegrated into a vague clearing with an indefinite horizon.

On the morning the chief of state finally arrived, the village was transformed into an exercise field for the maneuvers of various machines that serve to display military glory. Assault tanks, armored cars, and helicopters made the ground and the forest tremble, spreading the news to everyone within fifty kilometers or more that Zoaételeu and his vast family had been elevated to the ranks of pillars of the regime of the new chief of state.

He did not look like the great chiefs that could frequently be seen on television. He was not dressed in fatigues but in a charcoal blue suit cut from a fabric whose splendor and luxuriousness affected the patriarch's male children, who found out the following day that it was fine wool.

The chief of state wore a crimson tie that transfixed Zoaétoa and the other male children of the patriarch. Neither tall nor short, he was as stocky as Zoaételeu had been when, as a young man, he had engaged in the village brawls enthusiastically and to his advantage.

The chief of state, formerly the minister without portfolio, asked to see the quintuplets as well as the miraculous woman who had brought them into the world. The crowd of inhabitants, swollen by admirers from the neighboring villages, had gathered in the square when they heard of the chief of state's visit to Zoaételeu. The chief of state seized the opportunity to address the crowd, whom he delighted by speaking their language fluently.

"Everything was going badly for you up till now," the chief of state stated. "Everything will be better from now on, you'll see. I am what I am today thanks to your courage and to the unwavering trust with which you have favored me. That has been and will continue to be my strength. I know what you want, and I will give it to you because a sacred blood pact binds us, you and me. I will watch over you like a father over his children, better even than a father over his children. A new day is dawning, rich in brilliance and marvels of every sort for you and for your children. The others sought to harm you; they had taken away the venerable man who is your guide; they jailed him and, while he was imprisoned, they humiliated him. They dared profane that symbol of our timeless wisdom. As soon as I found out about this ignominy, I rebelled as I considered what our invincible ancestors would have done in my place. I said to those impious men, 'If you do not free this venerable old man immediately, misfortune will fall upon you like a vulture on a carrion.' They equivocated, they mired themselves like stinking jackals in a tangle of quibbling as endless as it was petty. So I unleashed the thunderbolts of retribution on those heathens. I overwhelmed them with a deluge of fire. I vanquished them. We are now the strongest. Our ancestors, wherever they may be, must be proud of us at this hour. That is the explanation of recent events. I sacrificed myself for your salvation. So let us walk hand in hand as our ancestors have always done. Let us renew the long-severed strands of our sacred solidarity, and we shall always be the strongest because we will always be the greatest."

The captain, who was part of the chief of state's retinue but who had craftily melted into the crowd, set off the applause and regulated the peasants' enthusiasm, gradually raising it from acclaim to ovation, with Zoaétoa's help. And it was also he who supplied the high point of this day of brotherhood when he shed his fatigues and started to dance in front of the populace, bare-chested, a loincloth tied around his waist, to the sound of the tom-toms. This time the villagers were expecting his performance. A deafening burst of tom-toms had greeted his first entrechats; behind him, a spontaneous trail of young men, led by Zoaétoa, and of young women joined him in the wild swaying; choirs of singers clapped in acknowledgment of the spinal torsion of the dancers. There was a general surge of joy and happiness that was gradually transformed into the delirium of reunion and communion in the ancestral culture.

"Let us leave our people to their happiness over our well-deserved victory over our enemies," the chief of state whispered in Zoaételeu's ear. "Let us retire to converse like the wise men of our ancestral tradition. Why does your son, Narcisse, willfully keep his distance from me? Is he unaware of all the trouble I went to, all the risks I took to save you once the situation became known to me thanks to Osomnanga? Do blood ties mean nothing to this young man who has a bright future provided he sides with me?"

The patriarch's boundless eloquence rose wonderfully to the occasion. This was the substance of his answer:

The Story of the Madman

"Great chief, you are surrounded by glory and splendor. Everyone bows before you, and yet you have come to me like a humble child seeking the shelter of his father's lap. I am proud of you, and the affection I feel for you is boundless. Ancestral tradition does indicate the path we should follow, but it is capricious Destiny that sets our itinerary. The man you have just named is, of all my sons, the one I have loved most dearly, and yet, he is not the one who obeys me most faithfully. I had chosen a fiancée for him. After refusing for a long time, he finally joined with her at my insistence and practically in front of my eyes. You already know the miracle she produced. It was a sign of concurrence from the ancestors; but Destiny chose otherwise. Great chief, Narcisse is more slippery than an eel; he is forever wriggling out of my hold. I do not even know where he is right now. Be Destiny; you have that power. Weave a net around this eel; take hold of this rebellious child and make him a man, I entrust him to you. As for me, I am probably too old. I have lived to see the passing of all my brothers, one after the other, and that of a large number of my sons, some in the cradle, others nearly adults. I have seen with my own eyes, on the screen, the torture of the colonel, a man who had shown me the most touching friendship, a son whose image of suffering remains a perpetual nightmare to me. I have lived through so many tragedies. I yearn now for the rightful repose of the exhausted warrior."

"What are you saying, oh venerable man?" answered the chief of state, deeply moved. "You are a miracle of nature, with your vigor, your endurance, and your wisdom. You will see all of us in our graves. Say no more about Narcisse. Leave him to me, I promise to bring him back to the fold. However, be assured of this: whatever happens, whatever Narcisse decides, your entire family is under my personal protection. Let anyone touch a hair on your head, or a hair on the head of a member of your family, and you will see the extent of my anger. May you and yours live in peace forever. It is the wish I make today, and Destiny is witness to my determination to make your happiness."

At dawn, after a night as sleepless for himself as for the villagers, who were overexcited by the celebration, the chief of state insisted on taking a ceremonious leave of these privileged constituents whom he called his brothers and sisters. He had them assembled in the square.

"My dear brothers, my dear sisters," he said in a voice that betrayed his fatigue but which was impregnated with a solemn firmness, "here are the decisions I have made in order to please you and to show you my extraordinary affection for you; from now on, your village will be a subprefecture, with all the attendant advantages of that status; the state will endow you with a school, a clinic, a post office, and a police station. The employees of these establishments will be chosen from among your children. The necessary funds will be allocated to you no later than tomorrow. I will personally watch over your prosperity. I count on you in turn to help me with all your strength."

Unable to gauge the value of the privilege being bestowed upon them, the peasants remained silent. The first sound of applause issued from the entourage of the chief of state at the initiative of the captain, who was still wearing a loincloth wrapped around his hips and whose bare chest was dripping with the sweat of the night's uninterrupted dancing. The peasants finally joined in, first by mimicry, then with the enthusiasm of simple masses subjected to the demagoguery of an adventurer.

That, at any rate, was how the lawyer interpreted the scene he and Narcisse witnessed incognito after they had arrived surreptitiously, late that night, and had hidden like fugitives in the bushes after leaving their Pajero* in the neighboring hamlet.

They had waited for the chief of state and his *smala*† to depart before coming out in the open.

"You must know that you should avoid compromising yourself with these people," the lawyer told the patriarch. "You would be exposing yourself to the vindictiveness of the politi-

---

*The Pajero was an eight-passenger, air-conditioned vehicle made in Japan. Possession of such a vehicle was a status symbol during the 1980s for the nouveaux riches and government officials.—*Translator's note*
†The group of tents that house an Arab chief with his family and following; by extension, a person's "tribe," family and followers.—*Translator's note*

cal leaders who will come after them. And they are not far be-hind. Already the opponents of the regime are readying their arms for the next putsch. Ask your son about it."

"Still, they are giving us a school and a clinic," Narcisse whispered, indecisively. "That's something."

"It is something, all right!" interjected Zoaétoa, who was present at the meeting.

"It is a poisoned gift, you idiot; don't you understand?"

"What do you think, Father?" Narcisse asked the patriarch.

"It's up to you to tell me," the old man replied after meditating on the subject for some time. "My children, I aspire for nothing more than my rest. You are the warriors now. Take up your lances and buckle your shields."

"You are the man who survived," the lawyer told him. "You are the oracle. Don't ever forget that. Your people expect you to tell them what to do. Tell them that they should avoid compromising themselves by siding with a tyrant, even if he is one of them."

"They would not obey him," Zoaétoa asserted.

"No, they would not obey him," Narcisse stated, rising to his elder brother's defense. "It's too late; everyone is too happy about getting a school, a police station, and a clinic, all free. Can you imagine? Free! And with all that, my father is going to come tell them, 'The clinic? The post office? The police station? We must give them all up, my children. We must refuse all this because politicians are dishonest people.' They would not understand."

"How do you know?" the lawyer asked. "Why must you always underestimate the common sense of humble people?"

As is typical for this corrupt country, Zoaételeu did not take the austere path advised by the eloquent and well-dressed young man who had defended him so spiritedly. The patriarch quickly succumbed to the pressure exerted by the impulsive, improvising, and impatient individuals who milled around him in as great a concentration as everywhere else in the republic. And so it was that new maledictions prowled around this unfortunate old man like hyenas with their tails between their legs.

THE LAWYER was truly a handsome fellow, and, furthermore, he did not dress like a dandy but like a respectable member of the middle class; although he was single, he did not venture from home after nightfall; he had never been known to have an affair with a married woman. He did not drink, he did not take drugs. And yet he could not persuade anybody. He did have the unfortunate habit of speaking Latin, having been raised in a religious institution. Malicious gossips—there are always bound to be some—claimed that unless one could jabber, if only a little, in this mythical language, one did not stand a chance of catching the attention of the young jurist. That was probably not the only reason for his lack of success among the political heads of the capital.

"*Hannibal ad portas! Hannibal ad portas!*"* they would shout in parody as soon as this cultured and perspicacious man entered a salon.

"Well, well, here comes the visionary!" a rival of the bar would comment in a low voice before greeting him with a thunderous, "Greetings, new Cassandra."

"You don't know how close you are to the mark, you poor devil," the lawyer would reply, his face serene though his words were tormented. In an aside, he would add: "*Urbem venalem et mature perituram, ubi emptorem inveneris.*"†

Someone would then ask him derisively, "Did the oracles

---

*Hannibal is at the gates!—*Translator's note*
†The corrupt and reprobate city where a buyer can be found (Sallust, *Bellum Jugurthinum* 35.10).—*Translator's note*

observe the flight of the black crows this morning? Have they predicted when this civil war you are forever harping on will occur?"

This obsession with an imminent civil war could also explain the vertiginous drop of the lawyer's credibility since the last coup. He was swimming against the tide of optimism that was making his fellow countrymen obstinate. He had predicted that the former chief of state would be executed as soon as he was sentenced by the military tribunal. The prisoner had not been executed, but neither had his sentence been officially commuted, and no one could answer for his successor's intentions. It was evidently only a pause in the bloody cycle of violence, but the thread of fatality had been severed, and the population rejoiced, so badly did everyone want a reason to rejoice finally after so many years of suffering and sadness.

The new chief of state, an apparently enigmatic man, had made no clear-cut decisions and had done nothing more than sprinkle his rare addresses with sensational but meaningless expressions such as renewal, moral tone, and austerity; these regularly echoed in the columns of government newspapers as well. That had been enough to win him the support and even the allegiance of several sectors of the populace, even among the tens of thousands of students on campus who were generally committed to a passionate intransigence.

Without actually sanctioning freedom of speech for the press, he had not interfered, and dozens of new titles had appeared, swelling the ranks of the clandestine newspapers that had already more or less staked out their claim. All these publications were hawked on the street or sold in newspaper stands, thus giving the military regime the engaging appearance of a democracy, and they were only seized from time to time if, for example, their impertinence touched on the strange situation in which the army was mired.

The regime's nervousness over the state of the armed forces led the lawyer to conclude that the new chief of state had only delayed the execution of his predecessor in order to barter the prisoner's fate for the surrender or voluntary exile of the air force and artillery corps commanders, who were entrenched in the North and in the western maritime region of the country.

"But, then," the political pundits in the capital objected, "that means that he is an old fox. He is a clever fellow, in fact, who, better than anyone, is aware that a civil war would ring the death knell of the republic. No, no, my dear man, that civil war of yours does not hold water; admit it, it is a chimera."

However, rumors circulated here and there, and not only in the lawyer's immediate entourage, that the dissident military leaders were preparing for a confrontation with the new leadership, and, judging from a number of patent clues, the latter was worried by the prospect. The rebels possessed a formidable arsenal that would allow them to sweep away the new chief of state and his troops in a matter of weeks, if not faster. They had not initiated open confrontations so far because they were unsure of the position of the former colonial power, since it had managed to keep its choice a secret, allowing each camp to believe that it had the western power's backing.

It was rumored here and there that, for the time being, the dissident officers were attempting to get to the bottom of the matter by sending delegation upon delegation to the president of the former colonial power.

"The one you take for a new messiah is a boa who is patiently winding its viscous coils around the populace in order to strangle it as soon as he can do so with minimum risk," the lawyer declared over and over . . . "and *jam bis medium amplexi, bis collo squamea circum terga dati superant capite et cervicibus altis.*"*

He had made a discovery that should have dampened his friends' hopes, but they had made up their minds once and for all to forgo skepticism. The new chief of state had secured the services of a well-known public works enterprise from the former colonial state to transform his palace, already designed

---

* Soon their scaly backs were entwined twice round his body and twice round his throat, their heads and necks high above him (Virgil, *Aeneid* 2.217–19, West translation).—*Translator's note*

like a fortress, into a sort of bunker. With a pair of binoculars, it was easy to verify that white workers, flanked by supervisors who were also white, were digging subterranean tunnels around the presidential palace and that machines disappeared into what were probably deep basements, reappeared, and disappeared again.

"This," the lawyer proclaimed, "is the symbol of what the regime must inevitably become. This man you admire so much today already has a single, driving obsession: to make his ouster impossible, to retreat literally and figuratively into an impregnable citadel. How do African despots obliterate all threats of replacement? Just look at Mobutu, my brothers, look at Sese Seko. Mobutu has three personal armies surrounding him, like three Great Walls of China, arranged in concentric circles around him. The interior wall is his presidential guard, made up of fourteen thousand men, all recruited from the villages and hamlets populated by his ethnic group, all very well paid and under the command of technical assistants from Israel. Next comes a sort of gendarmerie, also very well paid and led exclusively by Sese Seko's uncles, brothers, or cousins; finally, on the front line, to deal with riots and insurrections of the Zairean people, there is a sort of national security guard, less well paid than the previous troops but just as devoted. Within this sanctuary Mobutu lies entrenched; a triple-stranded Great Wall of China, bristling with fire-breathing muzzles ready to belch hell; no local force can dislodge him from there. As for the so-called national army, it is a horde of beggarly tramps without equipment, leadership, or pay, who are forced to hold the population ransom to survive. Our own Sese Seko is still constructing his bunker, then he will raise his private armies, three walls of fire, or possibly four or five, arranged in concentric circles, and nothing will be able to get to him. An eternal tyrant, in the political arena at any rate, is our one and only contribution to universal culture, as outsiders would say. Do you think that the events of 1789 would have occurred if Louis XVI had thought of safeguarding the institution of monarchy by divine right behind a Bastille such as this, a citadel at whose base all revolutions are doomed to flounder? Why do you insist

The Story of the Madman

on shutting your eyes, my brothers? Why must you always trust in miracles? . . . *ut ad bella suscipienda alacer ac promptus est animus, sic mollis ac minime resistens ad calamitates perferendas mens eorum est.*"*

Thus spoke the new Cassandra.

But no one wanted to believe the lawyer except Narcisse, who, moreover, followed him like his shadow to social gatherings, although he and Jeanne no longer needed a protector to lead the relatively luxurious life that he had dreamed of living for so long when he was a stray dog lost among the desperate hordes of hungry young urbanites. He had walked for so long in the wake of great men that the habit had grown on him, and he could not break free. It must be said that the jurist made no attempt to shake him off, quite the contrary; after all, was not Narcisse one of his best sources of information? Every time the latter returned from his village, which he often visited now pressed by his friend to fulfill his duties as father and husband, he would faithfully report what he had seen and heard to the lawyer.

The patriarch's educated sons, led by Zoaétoa, had fallen into the dictator's trap, and old Zoaételeu had been powerless to talk them out of the temptation of easy and abundant cash. These simple men had, until then, led a placid life that may have appeared, to the untrained eye, to be regulated by a disdain of gratification. But it was only the sluggish stirrings of unimaginative minds. There were ten of them. They were sent to a secret location in the capital to be trained. There they were taught how to create a cell for a political party, how to recruit members, how to stir unrest, and how, if necessary, to make a strike against rivals. These men, whose entire previous experience consisted of living in the woods, hunting with traps, frolicking in the river, and, on rare occasions, doing some ground clearing, received no other training.

They were given a large sum of money to build a new school

---

*Their spirits are eager and quick to undertake wars, so their minds are soft and least resistant to endure calamities (Caesar, *De Bello Gallico* 3.19).—*Translator's note* to replace the weather-exposed shed that had served that purpose. They proved incapable of managing it. They bickered, and it was all swallowed up without anyone's knowing exactly where it went. The ministry dispatched a construction team to build the post office, but the ten educated sons of the patriarch were kept away from the management of the money allocated for the building project. They were bitterly disappointed. Zoaétoa exchanged angry words with the European engineer in charge of the construction and kicked him bodily out of the village. Osomnanga had to come in person and only succeeded in settling the conflict by giving his most terrifying contortionist fakir performance.

Following that incident, the dictator sent for the three youngest members of the ten supposedly educated sons of the patriarch, which just happened to include Zoaétoa. He was the only one of the three to have reached the elementary certificate level, an exam he had failed four times before growing discouraged and quitting school. As for his two brothers, they had stopped over four years short of that level.

It had been so long since they had opened a book that they had become practically illiterate, like the rest of their brothers. Nevertheless, the dictator sent them abroad to receive accelerated officer training, according to rumor.

"Where do you think?" the lawyer had asked Narcisse.

"It's a secret; I think in Israel."

"Damn!" the lawyer had exclaimed. "It's not so surprising though, when you think of it. In any case, everything will have run its course here by the time they get back, and it isn't the dean of the diplomatic corps* who'll be able to do anything about it."

It was no longer a secret that high-ranking officers from both sides were meeting periodically, but these occurrences were barely mentioned in the newspapers or at social gatherings, where they were dismissed as folklore. Everyone could guess the reason behind these harmless conferences, especially since

*This is the official title of the ambassador of the former colonial power.— *Author's note*

they almost always took place at the embassy of the former colonial power. Its representatives assembled delegates from the two camps to attempt to work out a reconciliation. These negotiations failed one after the other.

The chief of state's representatives demanded that the dissident military leaders first return to the legitimate government, that is to say to the current chief of state, the planes, helicopters, and long-range missile launchers in their possession. The dissident leaders demanded that the former chief of state be set free first. The current chief of state suggested to the dissident military leaders that they leave the country, and if they settled abroad, he promised not to seek their extradition and to suppress inquiries into the funds that the military leaders, before becoming dissident leaders, had illegally appropriated, and generally into their various acts of extortion, which were being reported in detail in the columns of independent newspapers, causing them to be seized on a regular basis, only to resurface in the now well-worn clandestine circuits.

Then a rumor spread that, during a meeting which had once again taken place in the presence of the ambassador of the former colonial power, the dissident military leaders had dismayed both their mentor and their opponents by defying the current chief of state to organize free elections. What could have got into these men, famous for their narrow-mindedness, their group mentality, their complete indifference to populist fads, and their abhorrence of competition? Was their hatred for their opponents so intense that the only resolution they could suggest to the military ruling class was that of a collective suicide in an electoral free-for-all? everyone wondered in the air-conditioned anterooms of the embassy of the former colonial power. How could one continue to trust people so lacking in education and fair play?

This incident, which caught everyone off guard, was surely the trigger that led to the civil war the lawyer had predicted so often without ever convincing anyone. It is true that for a long time it remained insidious, latent even, like a cancer that gnaws away at an organism for a long time before the patient starts to feel the first symptoms.

The Story of the Madman

Blinded by its illusions, the elegant faction of the public sneered at these democratic pretentions coming from soldiers who were traditionally represented as the incarnation of fascist mentality. Fearful of losing its status as arbitrator, the embassy of the former colonial power confined itself to insinuating, to whomever wanted to hear, disenchanted assessments of the military faction opposed to the chief of state; moreover, it increasingly shed its hesitations about lifting its mask and positioning itself squarely as mentor of the only chief of state and his clan, which had the not-inconsequential effect of exacerbating the two camps' greater enmity.

The atmosphere suddenly grew stormy, and sarcasm directed at the military turned into grimaces when it was announced that the chief of state had applied to the International Monetary Fund and to the World Bank for help to bail him out of an impasse in the nation's finances that bore a close resemblance to bankruptcy. Apparently, the most pressing need was to settle the foreign debt, which amounted to a total never disclosed. It came out that the salaries of government workers, as well as those of employees of state-owned companies, would be affected the very next month. So many urban families whose daily needs had seemed completely assured for a long time to come, if not forever, were suddenly thrown into uncertainty and into the throes of unemployment and destitution. How could everyone have imagined that the fiscal crisis would not worsen here also as it had in all the other African republics previously colonized by the former colonial power?

The elegant circles of the capital finally stopped lampooning the man they had once dubbed the Cassandra of the shantytowns and turned to the lawyer to beg him to enlighten them. From one day to the next, he became the man who had foreseen. . . .

As usual, what was expected did not occur. Or rather, events unfolded in a way that surprised everyone. And yet the turmoil in the other African republics previously colonized by the former colonial power should have done away with any remaining illusions. But tragedies only happen to other people, as everyone knows.

The Story of the Madman

As the military crisis, instead of being resolved peacefully, was threatening to degenerate into open hostilities at any moment, despite the mediation, which was controversial besides, of the former colonial power, political turmoil erupted in a western maritime province. It became necessary to take action against a party that, boldly defying prohibitions and violating taboos, unleashed crowds of its fanaticized members into the streets. The chief of state dispatched troops that did not hesitate to open fire, several times, on processions of unarmed civilians and even on a group of children, leaving a large number of dead bodies strewn on the pavement on each occasion. Similar turmoil unfolded in other provinces.

Nothing like this had occurred since independence. The International Monetary Fund and the World Bank both pressured the chief of state to put an end to corruption, waste, and loss of capital resulting from fraud. They earnestly suggested that he allow honest and competent men into the government instead of his relatives, who crowded the ministries and treated their treasuries as their own personal funds. The chief of state did not act on these suggestions; he promised to think about it but flooded the cities with secret militias that spread a reign of terror as insidious as it was unpredictable.

On the advice of the former colonial power, which was skillfully playing several hands, the chief of state disingenuously decreed the freedom of political parties and of the press. In reality, he was in a state of panic and took back with his left hand what his right hand was forced to concede. Parties were formed, were legitimized, but were not allowed to hold public meetings or demonstrate in the street without risks, as the government invented a new pretext each time to muzzle them.

In the middle of this unprecedented fever, an inconceivable tragedy struck Zoaételeu the patriarch: the government newspapers announced that the quintuplets were dying, one after the other. There did not seem to be any way to stem this deadly sequence. The public barely remembered the skeletal and sickly old magus who had, in a way, crushed a tyrant through the admittedly unintentional prowess of his daughter-in-law. Even in circles where the government was hated, they pitied the old man,

The Story of the Madman

despite the fact that Zoaételeu was reputed to have joined the dictatorship and betrayed the people by agreeing to become a member of a commission of wise men frequently displayed on television by the chief of state, who claimed that he consulted them on every decision.

The lawyer persuaded Narcisse to visit his family only by agreeing to accompany him. He insisted that since Jeanne was bound to join them on the trip, her presence be handled with the extreme precautions required for this delicate situation. As soon as they appeared, the innumerable choir of wailers broke into the piercing cries of a sorrow that were no less heartfelt for being prescribed. In the middle of his people, the prostrated patriarch was bathed in tears, and his despair moved Narcisse and Jeanne to the core.

"My poor children, my poor children," the old man howled several times between two hiccups as he reached out to the newcomers. "My poor children. . . ."

The village was invaded by white shirts, by ambulances adorned with crosses, and by lugubrious-looking health workers. The quintuplets, the dead as well as the living, could not be seen. And besides, neither Narcisse nor Jeanne, who knew nothing of the ins and outs of the tragedy, nor even the lawyer perhaps, could have borne the sight of them.

"Only the chief of state will be allowed to see them," a specialist informed them. "He will arrive at any moment now. Meanwhile, we are under orders to save the two remaining babies at all costs, short of which we will be severely punished."

"Good God, what happened?" the lawyer asked. "And yet, they were saved; everybody said that after six weeks . . ."

"Oh, sir," the man in white observed, "you obviously do not know what quintuplets are like. There is nothing more fragile."

"They were surrounded by nurses, and even doctors—nothing was lacking!" Jeanne cried out, sniffling, swept despite herself into the collective sorrow.

"Oh, madam," said the specialist, crying bitterly, "who can ever say that nothing is lacking when it comes to quintuplets? An infection that would be benign for an ordinary baby in their case quickly turns into septicemia, then into an epidemic. And the next thing you know, all five are in agony. That is how it happened. There was nothing anyone could have done. By the time the nurses, as vigilant and devoted as they are, realized what was happening, it was too late. And there you have it. What a tragedy!"

"There are two left, you said?" the lawyer asked. "Those two will be saved at least?"

"Oh, sir, the odds are not good."

"Who are you, anyway?" the lawyer flared, suddenly annoyed and suspicious of this doctor who seemed to have forgotten his Hippocratic oath. "What are you? A marabout or a doctor with a university degree?"

"I am the chief of state's personal physician," the white-shirted man humbly replied.

"Oh, is that all!"

"Yes, sir, and he personally sent me here after the very first casualty. Believe me, we did everything that could have been done. But it is hopeless, I'm afraid. Oh, sir, what a tragedy!"

After distancing Jeanne, the lawyer convinced Narcisse to remain with his relatives. A man must support his family in a tragedy, he told him. And was not Narcisse the father, after all? It was up to him to preside over the traditional rites.

Nothing had prepared Narcisse for such an event. He hovered between terror and cold repugnance, not knowing to which temptation he could succumb without losing his dignity.

"Now, listen," the lawyer told him, "you can be a man for once, can't you? Go to your old father, comfort him. I have to leave you, man; you know why. I will return as soon as possible. Courage!"

When he returned three days later, the lawyer found Narcisse playing his manly role. He was going back and forth through the village, dispensing words of comfort, resolving petty quarrels among his relatives, handing out refreshments to the plethoric choir of wailing women, and giving directions to the grave diggers.

"Good job, man," the lawyer told him. "What about the mother, have you helped her also?"

"I'm sorry," Narcisse said, "but I have not been able to. I

can't, it's beyond my ability. And besides, think about it, there's Jeanne to consider."

"Forget it," the lawyer answered. "So how are the little patients? Did the chief of state come?"

"No," Narcisse replied.

"No wonder," said the lawyer. "He can't budge from his bunker, the poor guy. The whole country is in turmoil. Political parties are demonstrating everywhere and are calling for a national conference, like in Benin. Rampant groups are blocking roads all over some of the northern provinces. So the government denounces the bandits. In fact, the barely disguised dissident faction of the army is behind these skirmishes; I guess that this is its way of testing its opponents."

"And the former colonial power!"

"And the former colonial power as well."

"What is going to happen?"

"In my opinion, nothing. There is talk of an imminent military intervention by the former colonial power. That is our eternal curse. Will they ever leave us the hell alone? Still, I do not believe that will happen, not right now; it would not serve its darling's interests. There will certainly be articles in the press over there, surveys of public opinion and perhaps some debate. Personal jurisdictions would not hold up under scrutiny, you see. Private preserves are like latrines: you should avoid looking at them as much as possible."

The quintuplets had all died except for the eldest, who had been transported by helicopter to an American missionary hospital, located some two hundred kilometers away, the only medical facility in the country equipped for open-heart surgery.

"Father wants to see you," Narcisse told the lawyer. "Let's go."

The lawyer was looking all around him; he could not keep from being impressed, although, like all the men from the generation that came after the utopia of independence, he detested dictators and everything that reminded him of them: for one, he had known only foreign military interventions, psychopathic dictators, corrupt ministers, roadblocks, and elections that the single political party won by a 99.99 percent margin.

It seemed to him that, through the magic of power, the community had been living a sort of fairy tale before tragedy plunged it into mourning. Within an incredibly short time, the government had transformed a puny village, like a thousand others one can see along the roads in a single day's journey, into a busy town complete with many buildings and even public services, a post office, a school, and a police station run by one of the patriarch's sons following his return from a month's accelerated training in Morocco. On a spot where the forest was rapidly receding, something other than what had been was coming into existence.

"What about this?" the lawyer asked, pointing at an immense building under construction. "What is this monstrosity?"

"That is where the inaugural session of the oversight committee of the upcoming great political party will take place. It is, in fact, the future seat of the Party for Renewal, you see. What can I say, we are the fiefdom of the chief of state, so things have to be just so."

The patriarch was sitting in front of the blank television set, his eyes still bathed in tears, his gaze lost in the distance.

"Is that you, my son?" the old man asked, turning his head stiffly toward the lawyer, who was greeting him. "You know, since a few days ago, I can't see anymore. I was suddenly plunged into darkness. I was not expecting it. . . ."

"It's nothing, venerable one," the lawyer told him. "It can easily be treated. It is cataracts; it is operable even in elderly people."

"I don't know, my son. It is true that the chief of state's doctor told me the same thing. But why waste medical treatment on an old man whom the grave awaits impatiently? I wanted to say good-bye to you, my son, and to thank you again and again for everything."

"Who can say whether I won't go before you, old man?" the lawyer replied, without suspecting that he was, on this occasion, the most faithful oracle Destiny ever had. "Death is blind to age. Who can say who the next victim will be? Death spans all ages, so does life. Newborns, who seemed to have eternity before them, are dying."

The Story of the Madman

After overcoming so many trials, had the loss of his quin-tuplet grandchildren finally broken the patriarch's spirit? The young lawyer had almost drawn that conclusion, but Narcisse reassured him as soon as they were alone outside.

"Him, at the edge of the grave? You obviously don't know him very well. He will bury us all, you'll see. As for his sorrow, he will get over it. Believe me, he has lived through far more trying misfortunes. Still," Narcisse added, "it is gloomy here. The stench of death is everywhere because of these infants who were dropping like flies, without warning. It was horrible. It is not easy to forget. You are not going to leave me here again this time, are you?"

In reply, the lawyer confided something to Narcisse that would have momentous consequences for both of them.

"I have to leave the capital," he said. "I am no longer safe there the way things are going. I am going to join my friends in the great port. And you, what will you do?"

"I'm coming with you," Narcisse replied immediately. "We are coming with you, Jeanne and I."

So as to visit the patriarch Zoaételeu one last time before writing this chronicle, I managed to join a delegation made up of friends of Narcisse, who had recently died. They were going to report to the old man on proceedings they were undertaking, without recompense, to liquidate the young man's estate.

We were traveling in a convoy of three jalopies, and it so happened that I was in the same car as Jeanne, whom I did not know. I was immediately struck by the young woman's singular beauty but even more by her manner: her eyes were opened wide, and she was staring straight ahead; she sat stiffly and held her hand in front of her half-open mouth the way people suffering from nausea do.

She was silent. Someone was apprising her of the situation in a monologue that took up half the trip. I gradually understood that Jeanne was finally discovering the double life of her deceased companion, or that she was pretending to discover it, and was playing the role of the horrified companion, when she, of all people, must have had very few illusions about Narcisse's personality.

Over the hundred or so kilometers we traveled that day—not including the three hundred covered on the previous day between the great port, our point of departure, and the capital, where we met Jeanne—we encountered some thirty police roadblocks, where we had to stop each time, state our names, show our papers, and give the reason for our trip. The country was at the mercy of what, in retrospect, I can only call police anarchy. The former colonial power acted frantically behind the scenes, commissioned news articles full of the noblest allusions, hastily commissioned publications of the most erudite works imaginable, and generously financed television reports to glorify its protégé, the impression the chief of state projected about his position was not, as his powerful mentor would have wished, that of an Augustus founding a victorious and lasting dynasty, and even less that of a Louis XIV founding a form of government which, although despotic, was accepted if not desired in the very depths of the collective soul of the nation.

Everyone, and probably not least the chief of state himself, felt that he had condemned himself to the hell of a relentless, blind flight forward. As a crazy and interchangeable yet tragic puppet who was constantly having to put out the latest fire, he was compelled henceforth to keep resorting to the most revolting schemes, to multiply acts of brutal suppression, to alternate between crushing offensives and elastic retreats, to shift between the language of hate and that of reconciliation in one and the same breath, railing one day only to plead the next, and to hand out with the left hand what he took with the right, or vice versa.

And when you think about it, he was a man hounded by time just as a criminal is hounded by the police. It was impossible to imagine what good news other than trumped-up reports the passing days could conceivably deposit on the shores of his existence; on the other hand, it was only too clear what disasters the future was dispatching like a pack of baying dogs that, though still distant, was bounding full tilt toward him. By now everyone, except himself and possibly his protectors in the former colonial power, could sense that the destiny of this dictator, who so perfectly incarnated the blind stubbornness and inhumanity of the arrogant world whose instrument he was, would be to be broken one day against the wall.

Posterity will doubtless wonder how it had come to this, how so many people from so many different rungs of society, variety of positions, and wide range of latitudes could have fallen into this nightmarish trap.

As is usual in the tropics, the explosion of popular anger had taken everyone by surprise, including the experts, a faith-

The Story of the Madman

less breed that tends to resemble charlatans here, and who always receive noisy accolades while real scholars such as René Dumont preach to deaf ears. And these charlatans, breathless from spouting off, did not see the waters rising, even if we grant them the clairvoyance to perceive such things. Today, one does not have to be a sorcerer to be able to make out their shadows, rendered furtive and frantic by panic, lying trans-fixed in the basements of the bunker where the chief of state is holed up.

Of course, for a long time, for a very long time, there was only what could be compared to a barely visible trickle enclosed in a ravine that wound its way from far upstream and in which it seemed destined to remain trapped. This puddle laboriously infiltrated the tortuous anfractuosities in which it seemed likely to suffocate at any moment. Leaning over or on horseback above the precipice, like giants from afar, the charlatan experts hurled stones and guffawed as they counted the seconds that preceded the splash their projectiles made when they reached the bottom of the abyss.

"Opposition?" they exclaimed. "There would have to be political parties first. But there are no real political parties in Africa, only tribes. Opposition is an attribute of peoples; opposition, an eminently western concept, is completely alien to tribal mentality. Give me a Bob Denard, and I can hold Africa forever."

That was the waking dream in which the charlatan experts lived. And yet, over the decades, the brook has swelled with the cumulative bitterness of the urban population, the torrential impatience of generations, and the impetuous thrust of frustrated ambitions. One fine morning, as the sated experts lay sleeping in the downy beds of their irresponsibility, the deluge of time completed its work and the river overran its banks to charge toward the ocean.

Confronted with various concrete walls raised by despotism, the liberated tide regrouped and deployed its herds, the host of waves unfurled and their roar resounded farther than a bell. The fury of the tempestuous waves hammered away at the base of the edifice and shook it. Only then did the charlatan advisors abandon their rich kids' games.

The Story of the Madman

When a breach appears in the concrete of the dike, the chief of state's advisors entreat him to pool all his military resources, financial, human, and materiel, and stifle the monstrous gurgles as one would strangle an innocent traveler. When the turbulent waters begin to gush over the wall, the advisors convince the chief of state to raise it higher, however much it might cost him. So he orders the building of another wall upon the dike wall, as high as the original but twice as wide.

When the floodwaters hurled themselves at the flanks of the dike like a herd of elephants scaling the bulwarks of Kilimanjaro, the chief of state, at the advice of his charlatan advisors, and regardless of the cost, transformed the previously rectangular dike into an amphitheater, so that, faced with this rotundness, the roaring invaders found themselves momentarily powerless and were forced to retreat.

Into what new pharaonic prowess will the chief of state, more tireless than Hercules, be cornered through the advice of his charlatan advisors? The level of popular anger rises inexorably, the tide swells visibly. Now the chief of state and his advisors pray for the river to flow upstream. But everyone senses that this is a chimera. The chief of state and his charlatan advisors should have the wisdom to abandon this pointless madness in which they are thrashing, ruining themselves and ruining the former colonial state, the tutelary power, for rivers never flow upstream. Who can master waters that swell as they flow? The chief of state, his protectors, and his charlatan advisors have already lost the game. Who is going to tell them?

The chief of state and his various police forces maintained a feverish hold on the capital and its environs, which were considered part of his fiefdom, the province where the population, supposedly of the same ethnic group as he was, was presumably staunchly behind him. This paradox provided the opposition with a rich vein of sarcasm, along the lines that a husband who has his wife watched must be dubious of her continued faithfulness, assuming that he is not already a cuckold.

With an amazement akin to sadism, our convoy of jalopies witnessed everywhere an incredible swarm of men wearing green uniforms in public squares, on sidewalks, in the streets

The Story of the Madman

and villages, on country roads, and even in the heart of shanty-towns. Almost always drunk, sometimes to the point of un-steadiness, and displaying the arrogant and carefree demeanor of soldiers, they detained citizens, humiliated women and girls, misapprehended tax receipts, and stopped drivers, especially bus and taxi drivers, to hand them tickets that had to be paid on the spot with no guarantee that they would not have to pay the same ticket a hundred meters farther, ten minutes later.

It was not exactly the apocalypse: the flames and the embers of the last judgment were not visible anywhere, any more than were the streaks of lightning of a sky bursting open; thunder did not rumble along the horizon; cities kept on standing proudly, and their ocher walls seemed to continue bombastic, challenging the frothing of equatorial foliation on the immense stage of the republic.

Nothing actually collapsed; everything was turning in circles, but seemed frozen in some nauseous immobility. It was rather like the drowning of one of those insidious monsters that are said to have existed in prehistoric times: with its head submerged, it staved off asphyxiation by furiously splashing about, briefly emerging from the water only to sink back, flailing with every one of its slimy and glaucous tentacles that continuously buffeted the country with frothing walls of water. I understood why the late lawyer had anticipated, as if it were some extravagant carnival, this foaming debacle—this sullen shipwreck beneath a dull, wintry sky. The ogre who had spewed so much suffering on us for thirty years was now at death's door. For nobody doubted that these were the long-awaited death throes of the despotic regime—set up by the former colonial power in 1960 and gingerly supported by the latter ever since—defeated today less by the valor of its enemies than by the finally unveiled logic of its nonviable nature, like that of hydrocephalic babies. Like the lawyer, most of those who had sacrificed themselves to bring this day to pass had died and would never see it, having for the most part been devoured by this monster ever on the lookout for heads daring to protrude, in order to immediately sever them.

The observations that our trip afforded were supplemented

by countless newscasts on foreign radio stations. In the towns of the maritime provinces and particularly in the ports, rebellion rumbled through the population. Young people and the unemployed, two often indistinguishable categories, staged daily assaults on police stations, from which the occupants opened fire on them unrestrainedly. The rioters took hold of their dead and paraded down the streets, displaying them like trophies. Indignant crowds, swelling at each intersection, thronged around each body. This devastating tide then submerged one neighborhood after another, and it could be restrained by no obstacle except by darkness, in a city where lighting had been destroyed by riots, or by natural fatigue.

The distant provinces of the North had irrevocably pledged their allegiance to the dissident faction of the army. The latter proclaimed its peaceful intentions and its proposals in favor of nonviolence, but those responsible for blocking the roads had never been bolder, nor had they ever had a wider latitude in the area. According to unconfirmed and, moreover, quickly forgotten rumors, unidentified aircraft flew over the region gunning down columns of loyalist soldiers marching in unspecified directions. Without great success, the former colonial power persistently repeated its abjurations to the various parties, earnestly inviting them to the negotiation table.

The political parties that the chief of state had recognized, but which were in reality unwanted, gathered on private properties and composed heated motions calling on the chief of state to convene, at once, a fully empowered national conference, the necessary preliminary step, they proclaimed, toward the transition from a totalitarian dictatorship to the democratic and open governance of the republic.

Government employees had not been paid in three months. Furthermore, it was rumored that the International Monetary Fund and the World Bank had abandoned their negotiations with the dictator's government because the political restructuring they had insistently urged for some time now had not been forthcoming. As we entered Zoaételeu's village, the radio announced that the previous chief of state had been executed at dawn in that sinister quarry of the neighboring garrison town where he had previously ordered the massacre of other putschists. They said that he and his cronies had come to the same bloody end. They had been led in batches of seven to the execution posts. The frivolous young prosecutor had been in the same group of wretches as his boss; neither one of them had faced death with equanimity but had implored the executioners for mercy to the very end.

"It is hopeless!" one of the travelers in our group, doubtless a disciple of the late lawyer, observed.

A climate of intense partisan intolerance reigned in the patriarch's village, where we encountered only closed faces, shifty glances, and laconic replies; there was no doubt that we were unwelcome. Nevertheless, we had the privilege of an interview with the patriarch. He was now living in a large house worthy of a dignitary of the regime, with perpend walls and a corrugated metal roof instead of the traditional hut with its fissured walls showing spaces between blocks of packed clay. A few steps led to a veranda adjoined to a large living room, the only reminder of a communal tradition.

As if by design, the patriarch was holding an apparently healthy male child of about two on his knees when we arrived.

"He is the only survivor of my dear quintuplets," he told us looking both sad and blessed as he tickled the tiny tot, who finally broke out in giggles. "Perhaps you would like to see the mother? She is probably taking care of some chore in the forest. If you wait a few hours, you'll see her, she will be back by then."

"She is back," an adolescent hidden in a dark area of the living room volunteered.

"Go fetch her," his grandfather ordered.

"Those ladies will be annoyed to have their dancing interrupted for no good reason," the adolescent said.

"What is the occasion for this dancing?" one of my traveling companions thoughtlessly inquired.

"What is the occasion for this dancing?" the patriarch repeated, trying to sound amused. "Do women ever need a pretext to dance, my son? It's easy to see that you are from the city. Isn't dancing the raison d'être of these creatures just as reproduction of the race is that of the animals of the other sex? As long as women arouse men, nothing is lost and Zambo Menduga's lineage will continue on its merry way, thank God."

The meeting lasted two long hours, during which, deaf to what was being said, I observed the still alert old man holding his grandson on his knees, the only survivor of a litter both miraculous and cursed.

What was the secret of his surviving so many hazards? This question, which I was not incapable of answering myself, nevertheless obsessed me, and I felt a sudden urge to put it to him. I had lost my familiarity with the language, and I silently searched in vain for the words I would use to question him. Suddenly, I was unexpectedly moved to the very depth of my being not by the substance of the predictable maxim he had just articulated but by the serene faraway tone in which he had said it, and I had the intuition that I was getting closer to what I had come looking for, unless it had already been given to me without my realizing it. Abruptly, the old man broke a long silence and, seemingly out of nowhere, declared, "Yes, Zambo Menduga used to say that as long as women arouse men, nothing is lost."

He had repeated this adage three or four times before I began to understand it. The old man was in the habit of attributing to his ancestor, the famous Zambo Menduga, whose epic seems to have been unknown to everyone except the patriarch Zoaételeu, his descendant in the thirty-first generation, truisms that the ancestor had perhaps never articulated but which, through this means, acceded to the dignity of revelations.

The only secret to his survival, then, was the very same one that had continued to amaze me since my discovery of the history of our people, because without it so many Africans all over the world would not have survived the slave trade, bondage, the ravages of colonial conquests, Blood River, various kinds of segregation, colonization, and now the psychopathic dictators in their carved-out private domains. In each case, the survival of the race had been ensured by the male's fury to reproduce. It was our only strength. And, finally, the lawyer acknowledged as much when he gave the directive that has remained enig-

The Story of the Madman

matic to skeptics and stupidly demagogic to dogmatists: *Hold tight, survive until the year 2000. And then* . . . Zoaételeu said the same thing but in different words, or rather did not say it but certainly showed it by organizing his little world in such a way as to make reproduction the one overriding concern and ensuring that everyone held the group's survival above that of the individuals. He too must have been thinking, although more nebulously than the lawyer: *Hold tight, survive. And one day* . . . But what day? And what of that day? That, he could not have said except with myths or legends that would have caused much hilarity among skeptics and demagogues, who would be in agreement for once.

As for him, he was obsessed with Narcisse's death. He insisted on being told the circumstances in detail. Jeanne resolved to comply with his wish, after hesitating for a long time because her friends, speaking in French so as not to be understood by the patriarch, were advising her against it.

She resolved the dilemma by warning the old man that she did not know all the facts. This ruse allowed her to feel free to hide the most important part: the most important part was also the most dreadful part, news of a kind that could possibly have caused the patriarch to die of horror and despair had he known it.

So HERE ARE the appalling circumstances under which the lawyer and Narcisse died, united to the last.

For a long time, the great port had appeared to be a fiefdom of the dissident faction of the army just like the rest of the maritime provinces. That was not the case in fact; while keeping up the illusion of a presence there, the usually silent dissident faction of the army had pulled its forces out in order to concentrate them around a few bastions located in the far North, and only the chief of state's uneasy conscience, in conjunction with an instinct for procrastination, had engendered and spread this belief, which alone could explain why government partisans did not venture into the great port after the successful coup. For all that time, the city was left to its own devices.

Workers unions, radical groups of all kinds, associations of young unemployed persons, pop artists trying to be prophetic, and extravagant religious sects had taken it over and ruled it. Every day had its demonstrations, its chorus of solidarity with oppressed women, its prayer meetings, its expositions of masterpieces from regional cultures accompanied by tribal dances.

Leaders of civilian opposition came to this island of liberty from the four corners of the country to hold political meetings that sent echoes overseas, infuriating the chief of state, although his radio and television stations never mentioned them, except to dispatch loyal journalists who acted mostly as spies.

It was upon reading a report by one of these duplicitous men, describing the recent formation of a union of opposition parties and its alleged diabolical and undoubtedly criminal hold

The Story of the Madman

on the great port's crowds, that the chief of state resolved to regain control of the town and its inhabitants. However, he had planned a tactical retreat in the event that the dissident faction of the army, suspected of having deliberately abandoned the great port to subversion, attempted to interpret this maneuver as a provocation and used it as a pretext to return to the great port in full force; he had no intention of engaging his formidable enemies in an uncertain confrontation on their own turf. Furthermore, he had not received permission to do so.

The advance forces of the loyalist faction in the great port were composed solely of clandestine, multipurpose units dressed in civilian clothes. Suddenly, police stations, municipal administrative offices, public buildings, and the headquarters of large companies swarmed with men in green. They ventured to strut along the sidewalks, the main squares, and the public gardens with an arrogance they attempted to hide but without much success.

Children threw stones at them in front of the entrances of deserted schools, where odd crowds now congregated. Tall male inhabitants changed course, turned back, or crossed the street to come face to face with them and to spit in their faces before insulting them in the foulest terms. They say that a woman of loose morals, who had openly removed her panties, proceeded to march in step with a column of uniformed men, regaling them with the less-than-attractive spectacle of what is commonly known as the padded part of the anatomy.

What was bound to happen happened: an officer in the chief of state's tribal militia, fresh from a training course in Israel and possibly a little tipsy, opened fire with his machine gun on a gang of young boys who were taunting him. A riot ensued that lasted two days and two nights and resulted in several dozen deaths on both sides.

The chief of state made a televised statement castigating the agitators and swore to preserve public order at any cost. The union of opposition parties published an incendiary statement that concluded with its commitment to work with all its strength, in concert with other fraternal organizations, to help rid Africa of mad dictators.

This was a new front along which the chief of state was forced to fight. He did so in his own way: he hurriedly managed to erect around his person those three lines of human ramparts so often but unconvincingly predicted by the lawyer, which effectively sheltered the dictator from any possible surprise. Israeli bodyguards made up his personal guard; an elite regiment, considered the official presidential guard and headed by his eldest son, occupied the capital continuously; a third buffer force, based near the chief of state's native village and made up of parachutists, was a rapid intervention unit that had acquired an embryonic air force fleet furnished, crew and maintenance included, by the former colonial power using Israel as a front.

It appeared that the chief of state's seat of power had become an impregnable citadel, beyond the reach of popular uprisings at any rate.

Rumor had it that the chief of state now had enough ammunition and provisions in the basements and caves of his palace to hold out for several months, in the purely academic eventuality of his various armies' being defeated and all his lines of defense being breached.

Short of defying his adversaries in the dissident faction of the army, which was now squarely entrenched in the North and patiently watching him for signs of fatigue, this timorous man unleashed squadrons of terror, trained in the best schools, on the restless civilian crowds of the cities, particularly those of the great port. The latter slowly slid into urban guerrilla warfare, with its well-known cycles of acts of aggression by rogue elements followed by bloody reprisals by law enforcement forces, so that its days belonged to government agents and its nights to their civilian adversaries, with isolated members of the police being executed in retaliation for assassinations allegedly committed by the forces of law and order. When, to top it all, the union decreed official days of civil disobedience, all hell broke loose. Amazingly, none of this leaked to the outside world, especially not in the news coverage by the former colonial power.

Unable to endure his helpless exasperation any longer, the

The Story of the Madman

chief of state decided to resolve the matter; he had all the leaders of the opposition arrested simultaneously, in their respective homes, early one morning, or so he thought initially. He was wrong. Only a few of them were in the city. Those who were caught were taken to an unknown destination, as the saying goes; they were beaten to a pulp all day, and some were cruelly tortured. But they were all set free the following day by order of the minister of foreign affairs of the former colonial power, acting through the intermediary of his ambassador. The dictator's armed takeover had been reported by one of London's leading newspapers, and a scandal seemed imminent. This was all in vain, but it engendered an iron resolve among the leaders of the opposition.

In October of that year, the union of opposition parties, in their sanctuary on the grounds and outlying buildings of a private villa, held a general assembly in the great port. The meeting lasted twenty-four consecutive hours and attracted many gawkers, who were particularly hard to weed out because they usually claimed to be journalists and self-confidently presented their press passes. Many were skillful spies; a government assassin, concealed in the crowd, observed the orators and took feverish notes in a gold-edged notebook.

From time to time, he got up and, clutching his stomach as if he were suffering from indigestion or from any other similar complaint, pretended to go to the bathroom. He locked himself in a stall, pulled out a miniature radiophone from a holster, and proceeded to communicate with his project officer, located a few kilometers away in a police station or in a very ordinary-looking vehicle.

It was indeed a feast for the chief of state's many spies, who were spread out incognito in the audience, for the union had wanted to make a statement, and all its noteworthy figures were there, including some who were already known abroad and others less well-known but no less fascinating to the great port's crowds who idolized them.

On stage, in the wings, and in the large reception halls of the private villa hosting the union's event, the wide white boubous of the North mingled in fraternal enthusiasm with jeans, with the bush shirts of the South, and with the embroidered robes of the coast. Every province, every social class, every occupation, and every generation was represented. It was a preview of the democratic parliaments of tomorrow. In addition to politicians riding the crest of popularity, there were also national and African celebrities from the literary and entertainment worlds.

The union took advantage of this occasion to mark a decisive turn in its strategy; it appointed a president, a secretary-general, a treasurer, and a spokesman, who would henceforth represent it everywhere and speak in its name. The following day, this innovation would be hailed by the independent press, which was increasingly regressing to a clandestine state, as a triumphant step toward the formation of an empowered national conference at a decisive moment in the history of the nation; it did, as a matter of fact, cause the chief of state's entourage—whose ranks had recently been joined by a certain Zoaétoa, son of Zoaételeu, a man hallowed with promise and lately returned from an accelerated training course in Morocco—to initiate a long-planned operation.

The newly elected president of the union was a thin man with a serious face and melancholic and intelligent eyes—perhaps too intelligent, since he would soon prove to be a virtuoso of double-dealing, negotiating his collaboration with the dictator at the same time as he was spouting off his diatribes and parading on the stages of the rebellion. He thanked his comrades in a speech that was as short as it was severe on the chief of state, whom he accused of walling himself up in his refusal to convene an empowered national conference, which would take place anyway, since the people wished for it unanimously.

"Consult the history of nations," he proclaimed. "It will teach you, and it never errs, that the people have always prevailed in the end, over the obstinacy and blindness of tyrants."

This ingenious reprimand, in which everyone thought they recognized the lawyer's hand but which, in fact, was a take-off on the Convention delegate Saint-Just, was unanimously applauded, *ut barbaris moris, fremitu cantuque et clamoribus dissonis** muttered the lawyer.

*As with barbarian ways, murmuring, cackling, and confused shouting (Tacitus, *Agricola* 33.1).—*Translator's note*

The Story of the Madman

And yet the target of the chief of state's assassin was not the president but the lawyer, who had become the anathema of the intimate circle of the dictator. Behind the scenes and at center stage, he had been the driving spirit behind this conference of the union and the architect of the success of the assembly; it was he who had succeeded in thawing the usually anxious delegates with redundant half pathetic, half clownish tirades invariably sprinkled with Latin quotes. And when necessary, he had deployed historical references or concepts of high philosophy, which though not always very sensible were always meticulously documented, to render audacious decisions acceptable to intellects who had become circumspect and even timorous through a conjuncture of madness.

Unaware that he was, in a way, delivering his own testament, he had uttered these extraordinary words, which would haunt those who heard them for a long time and in which I myself believed I had found the title of this modest chronicle:*

"Hold tight, comrades. Persevere and Africa will finally crush the hydra that has been tormenting it since the beginning of time. Follow the example of that modern messiah, Nelson Mandela, who has just been released from prison, prevailing with his people after a half century of indescribable suffering. Survive until the year 2000, and then a wonderful world will open before you. Large, prosperous cities await you. I see in the distance monuments erected to the glory of our heroes, fields covered with crops as far as the eye can see, proud populations marching happily and freely on the soil of the ancestors. *O passi graviora, dabit deus his quoque finem. Durate, et vosmet rebus servate secundis.*† The third millennium will witness the apotheosis of our beloved Africa, the crowning of our struggle. Destiny has so willed. *Aspera tum positis mitescent saecula bellis.*‡ Survive, I say, survive until the year 2000 and then . . ."

---

*Survive to the year 2000! Unfortunately, another title was chosen!—*Author's note*

†My friends, this is not the first trouble we have known[,] we have suffered worse before and this too will pass. [. . .] Your task is to endure and save yourselves for better days (Virgil, *Aeneid* 1.198–99, 207, West translation).—*Translator's note*

‡Then wars will be laid aside and the years of bitterness will be over (Virgil, *Aeneid* 1.291, West translation).—*Translator's note*

The Story of the Madman

As absurd as it may seem, his most unpardonable crime in the eyes of the chief of state's close advisors was simply that of influencing Narcisse to distance himself from *his people* and making of him an example that was liable to weaken the allegiance of his brothers and others like them. Having exhausted its resourcefulness and stratagems, the sole remaining recourse left to the chief of state's circle was to divide the various national communities by initiating and exacerbating hollow quarrels between them in the hope of delaying its own ruin.

The assassin shadowed the lawyer from the moment the delegates and their crowds of innocent admirers dispersed. He would stick to him till the end. It was an easy mission, on one of the rare sunny days of the season after weeks of practically uninterrupted downpours and storms in the city. There was a dense crowd of pedestrians everywhere, even on the broad avenues of the old European residential city where there are neither restaurants nor commercial establishments lining its streets but only white colonial villas, standing some distance from each other and shaded by the permanent foliage of mango and coconut trees.

The lawyer, driving his Pajero himself as usual, made a stop in this neighborhood and waited for someone to open the gate of a villa recessed from the road and hidden behind a clump of giant flowers. The assassin's car, which had been closely shadowing the Pajero, broke free and passed it slowly, but accelerated suddenly as if an unexpected obstacle, possibly the guard coming to open the gate, had appeared.

It was well into the night when the lawyer finally left the villa; his Pajero looked practically like a bus with all the people who had boarded it, including some very young children. It traveled a long time, crossing the old European city and stopping several times to drop off passengers; finally, it entered a picturesque quarter made up of poorly lit alleys that intersected each other at right angles, and stopped in front of a large villa enthroned in the middle of a debacle of poky little houses set haphazardly all around. The car stood still for a few dozen seconds that seemed an eternity; the double gates finally opened

The Story of the Madman

wide and swallowed the Pajero. It was the residence of a high-ranking official now in disgrace; he was hosting a party in honor of the only English-speaking leader of the union, a man whose rare integrity, in stark opposition to the general corruption, already destined him to the ever-growing adoration of his fellow countrymen, before, soon thereafter, making him the only opposition leader capable of throwing the chief of state's entourage into a panic and perplexing its foreign protectors. The lawyer and Narcisse had agreed to meet here because the latter, who was now passing himself off as a businessman, hated political rallies and was waiting there for the lawyer, his inseparable friend at whose side he would meet with a revolting and absurd end.

The dinner and the congratulations lasted past midnight. The lawyer was never more brilliant, as if he wished to ensure that his friends would be made desolate by the loss of such an incomparable man, a scholar, a militant, a prophet, and a knight always ready to protect the weak. He addressed a tribute in Latin, based on the one composed by Tacitus for Germanicus, to the English-speaking guest being honored. Even though they had not understood a single word, the audience, made up mainly of nouveaux riches and uneducated bureaucrats, with the exception of the English-speaking politician himself, who was a bookseller by trade and creditably lettered, applauded loudly and at great length.

Narcisse, who had a low tolerance for alcohol, had gone on ahead to the Pajero and had lain down in the backseat as usual. On such occasions, the lawyer took care not to wake him; he took him straight back to Jeanne, who had been trained to leave their house gate ajar with a guard posted at the entrance all night. That is what the lawyer was going to do when the party hosted by the out-of-favor high official came to an end.

Having arrived last, he had to leave the garage of the out-of-favor high official first to make way for the other guests.

The lawyer and Narcisse, who was sleeping in the Pajero's backseat, never reached Jeanne's side. Exasperated by his subordinate's evasions, the project officer had decided to finish the job himself. Lurking in the corner of an alley, he had waited and kept watch. The Pajero gingerly extended its large high-riding nose toward the edge of the purple streaked pavement; a harmless passerby, looking somewhat ridiculous in a getup that included shades, an improbable cap, a movie pirate's head scarf across his forehead, and a gray raincoat, approached slowly. He was whistling a popular tune. Stopping by the driver as if to ask the lucky bourgeois for charity, he suddenly lifted his arm and threw a grenade inside the Pajero. That passerby, disguised as a harmless and ridiculous bum, was none other than Captain Zoaétoa, son of Zoaételeu, Narcisse's very own brother and an officer in the special commandos corps of the presidential guard, who had just returned the previous week from an accelerated training course in Morocco.

The Pajero made an apocalyptic leap and disintegrated on its way down, shattering the night with the blast of the explosion and a deluge of metal. Its occupants had been blown to bits.

*Durate, et vosmet rebus servate secundis.** Survive until the year 2000! The lawyer had not had the wit to follow his own instructions; he would never live the marvels that the promised land of liberty was finally to lavish on Africa. At least he had been able to see the liberation of Nelson Mandela, and that had made him inexpressibly happy.

---

*Your task is to endure and save yourselves for better days (Virgil, *Aeneid* 1.207, West translation).—*Translator's note*

JEANNE CHOSE NOT to reveal the identity of the executioner to the wretched old man whom she considered her father-in-law, although he never actually was. She herself only found out during the trip and was still reeling from the shock.

Yet Zoaételeu will have to learn one day, probably soon, that his idolized son was assassinated, innocently in a way, by another of his too numerous sons. On that day, he will perhaps understand that the fundamental principle of his philosophy was erroneous or, at least, incomplete: where there is an abundance of children, there is not only an abundance of generosity but a greater abundance of grief and sorrow.

Before joining the service of the chief of state, Zoaétoa, like his other brothers, had been saddled with several wives by his father; they had given him, as the expression goes, several children of both sexes, all still very young, whose education, in the peasant tradition, has been assumed by their grandfather. As a result, they hardly miss the man who fathered them.

On the other hand, Zoaétoa's wives are beginning to clamor for their man, from whom they have been separated too long for the deprivation not to be painful; they come whisper their recriminations to the old man, who lends them a willing ear. They say that if absence is justifiable, abandonment is sacrilegious.

Zoaételeu will soon have to send for his son Captain Zoaétoa, officer in the special commando corps of the presidential guard, who has not visited his family since he engaged in the chief of state's army. First he used distance as a pretext, then the endless duties of his training. During his instruction abroad, he did not even deign to write to his family, and was overjoyed to have a foolproof excuse.

Zoaételeu will find out that, immediately upon his return to the country, his son Zoaétoa, captain in the special commando corps, unknowingly assassinated Narcisse, the son he cherished above all others, that since then Zoaétoa's too fragile soul was unable to survive the discovery of the nature and extent of his crime.

But perhaps Zoaételeu will never know the truth. They will send word to the patriarch that his son Captain Zoaétoa, officer in the special commando corps, disappeared without a trace in that great port where so many people disappear without a trace. Zoaétoa, son of Zoaételeu, noble offspring of the illustrious lineage of Zambo Menduga and of men each more valorous than the last, will doubtless rot in the midst of the refuse where he rummaged for his miserable sustenance, and passersby will hold their noses without so much as a backward glance for what they will take to be the carrion of some wandering animal.

Perhaps Zoaételeu will never know the truth and will remain convinced that where there is an abundance of men, there is necessarily an abundance of generosity.

Afterword

Mongo Beti is a major and long-standing figure of French-speaking African literature and an enduringly principled intellectual. His radical thinking illuminates the colonial and postcolonial conditions, in Africa and in Cameroon. Uncompromisingly faithful to his ideals, he has put himself on the line and earned the respect owed to those who stand in the way of injustice and obscurantism. To younger generations of Cameroonians fighting for democracy, he is a point of reference and a role model.

Alexandre Biyidi-Awala (Beti's real name) was born in June 1932 in Akometam, a village twelve kilometers from the city of Mbalmayo, in Cameroon's "centre-sud" region. Expelled from the Catholic mission for "insubordination," he entered the lycée in Yaoundé, the country's administrative capital, where he received the French baccalauréat in 1951. That same year he arrived in France to pursue his studies at the Université de Provence. He had a French passport and was the recipient of a fellowship from the Ministère de la France d'Outre-Mer (formerly, Ministère des Colonies). Provided he passed two exams within two years, he was permitted to go back home, on vacation. He did so and remained until the late 1950s, when the repression of opposition, notably against the UPC (Union des Populations du Cameroun, formed in April 1948), intensified, and the UPC's secretary-general, Ruben Um Nyobè, was killed in September 1958. Like most Cameroonian students at the time, Biyidi sympathized with the UPC, and although never one of its formal members, he worked in favor of the opposition party.

Afterword

Mongo Beti remained in exile in France for thirty-two years, from 1959 to 1991. This was particularly painful when the political pressures following the first publication and consequent censure of his essay *Main basse sur le Cameroon: Autopsie d'une décolonisation* (Stronghold on the Cameroon: Autopsy of a decolonization) in 1972 cut him off from his beloved mother, with whom he was unable to communicate for almost three years.[1] Returning to Cameroon then meant either rallying to the government in power and serving its (and neocolonial France's) interests or being jailed and risking his life. Deciding to stay away, Beti may appear to have chosen exile, but there were no viable alternatives in his eyes: "Had I gone back and declared that [Ahmadou] Ahidjo was the most impressive and the greatest, they would have re-integrated me into the system, but I would have been unable to survive like that, because I am incapable of hiding my feelings."[2]

In 1959 Beti began a career in teaching. He received the CAPES (Certificat d'Aptitude à l'Enseignement Secondaire) in Paris, which enabled him to teach in the French educational system at the secondary level. In 1966 he and Odile Tobner, his second wife and the mother of their three children, passed the selective Agrégation de Lettres Classiques and were appointed in Rouen; he, at the Lycée Corneille, where he worked until he retired in 1994, and she, at the Lycée Jeanne d'Arc.

Beti's literary career began when he was a student. A chapter of his novel *Ville cruelle* (Cruel city) was published in the journal *Présence Africaine* in 1952, under the title "Sans haine, sans amour" (Without hate or love). *Ville cruelle* was published in 1954 under his first pseudonym, Eza Boto. His second novel, *The Poor Christ of Bomba,* came out in 1956, under the pseudonym of Mongo Beti, which he was to use in all subsequent works. *Mission to Xala,* for which he was awarded the Prix Sainte-Beuve, and *King Lazarus* quickly followed, in 1957 and 1958.

Mongo Beti married Odile Tobner, his frequent collaborator, in 1963. From 1958 to 1972, he dedicated himself to his family and his teaching career. In 1972, after a fourteen-year span, he resumed writing with the political essay mentioned above, *Main basse sur le Cameroun: Autopsie d'une décolonisation.* This dense volume was written in reaction to the arrest, trial, and conviction by the Ahidjo government of Ernest Ouandié, president of the UPC, and Albert Ndongmo, Nkgonsamba's Catholic bishop and a popular figure in the opposition.[3] It marked a turning point in Beti's life and literary production. The extensive research he conducted on his country broadened his knowledge, sharpened his political judgment, and gave radical meaning to his exile. It clarified and grounded his position as an African intellectual facing such questions as that of independence.

Main basse also confirmed the original direction of Beti's creativity. Deeply rooted in history, it combines fiction and social commentary through essays, articles, and even a dictionary. It converges into a pluralistic body of work held together by a strong internal logic: the figuring (out) of postcolonial politics, that world where "reality goes beyond fiction" (*Main basse* 11).[4] Attempting to grasp, decode, and expose the "world of madness" (*Main basse* 13) that is the postcolonial state, Beti's writing has both a moral and investigative quality. It expresses a strong imperative for truth, freedom, and social justice, and an idealism rooted in a keen observation of real-life situations, in Africa and abroad.

The first publication of *Main basse*, in 1972, by François Maspéro's left-leaning publishing house, resulted in a four-year judicial battle against the French government. Highly critical of the Ahidjo regime and of France's grip on Cameroonian affairs, the book was censured by Georges Pompidou's interior minister, François Marcellin, who ordered the book seized. The French government also tried to strip Biyidi of his French nationality, but the writer eventually succeeded in warding off the threat. In 1976, the censorship was revoked, with apologies, and Maspéro issued a second edition of *Main basse*. A third edition followed in 1984 by the Éditions des Peuples Noirs, the establishment Beti and Tobner had set up in 1979, the main purpose of which was to publish their journal *Peuples Noirs-Peuples Africains.*

The next two novels to appear, *Perpetua and the Habit of Unhappiness* and *Remember Ruben,* were the direct consequence of the *Main basse* affair. These two volumes came to form a "chronique rubéniste" with the addition of *Lament for an African Pol,* published in 1979.

Another chronicle followed, made up of *Les deux mères de Guillaume Ismaël Dzewatama, futur camionneur* (The two mothers of Guillaume Ismaël Dzewatama, truck driver to be) (1983) and *La revanche de Guillaume Ismaël Dzewatama* (The revenge of Guillaume Ismaël Dzewatama) (1984), and featuring the adventures of a biracial, Franco-Cameroonian family. Since then Beti has published three novels, *The Story of the Madman* (1994), *Trop de soleil tue l'amour* (1999), and *Branle-bas en noir et blanc* (2000).

Between 1984 and 1994, when *The Story of the Madman* came out, Beti produced two political essays, *Lettre ouverte aux Camerounais ou la deuxième mort de Ruben Um Nyobè* (An open letter to Cameroonians or Ruben Um Nyobè's second death) (1986) and *La France contre l'Afrique: Retour au Cameroun* (France against Africa: Return to Cameroon) (1993), in which he takes stock of his country's evolution upon his return, in March 1991. During that time he and Tobner, together with other *Peuples Noirs-Peuples Africains* collaborators, had also compiled the *Dictionnaire de la Négritude* (Dictionary of negritude) (1989).

Beti's literary creed has not fundamentally changed over the years. Discussing the future of French-speaking African literature, in "Afrique noire, littérature rose" (Black Africa, rose-colored literature) (1955: 134–35), Beti underlined three major ideas that would influence his entire writing career: the prevalence of the novel, the necessity of realism versus a politically tamed picturesque, and the importance of "personality," or moral character, in the author. From the beginning, Beti considered realism a historically required, revolutionary tool in the fight against colonialism. Later, after independence, when his fears about France's retaining control over its ex-colonies were confirmed, Beti assumed the same creative fighting stance against neocolonialism.[5]

Aiming to convince the reader, Beti's writing is didactic and rhetorical. Constructed as a causal system, it is elaborately built up, and it highlights hierarchical relations through frequent use of subordinate clauses. Betian sentences can be lengthy. They are tightly woven with striking images whose rhythm is marked by a controlled use of punctuation. Beti uses broad strokes to sketch his characters. In a technique reminiscent of that of a writer he frequently refers to, Victor Hugo, he concentrates on generic traits to construct an exemplum, or exemplary narrative.

Beti's writing is informed by a critical awareness of the hegemonic status of the French language and culture, in French-speaking Africa in general, and in Cameroon in particular. One of the characteristics of his oeuvre is its preoccupation with, and subtle representation of, the fault lines of language. In *Madman,* that practice is evidenced when Narcisse and the colonel address one another, in French, in front of a bemused Zoaételeu: "The patriarch was as intrigued by the poignancy of the gestures and facial expressions as by the enigmatic sounds of a language to which he had never had any access" (37).

The picturing of such talking at cross-purposes is an intrinsic part of the Betian narrative. From the beginning of his career as a novelist, Beti has played on different linguistic and semantic registers. He has made use of Latin, Bantu, and Pidgin expressions, together with a system of echoing (and ironic) footnotes, to problematize the linguistic situation of his country as well as the restrictive nature of his narrative tool: French. His inclusion of Latin quotations is not new to *Madman*; this method is featured elsewhere in his fiction, in *Ville cruelle,* Beti's first novel, for example. In that book, French is used to communicate the opacity of Latin, the language of Catholic liturgy and religious dogma, as well as that of the European agents of colonization in Africa: the missionaries. Latin, once the dominant language of culture in Europe, is criticized through French, the language of cultural domination in French-speaking Africa.

Afterword

The use of both Latin and French highlights the absence of the protagonist's (and the writer's) native language: Ewondo. They forcibly, but indirectly, refer the reader to the linguistic and semantic gap informing the young Cameroonian's (colonial) reality. The back-to-back use of the two dominant languages serves the dual purpose of underlining the arbitrary nature of foreign ideologies and authority figures and, through the figure of the catechist, of alerting Africans to the dangers of political sedateness. Banda's persistent state of confusion therefore aims at "telling" people in his situation that they do not have sufficient grasp of their lives and should do something about it. In turn, *Madman* highlights the metonymic relationship between Latin and Rome to deliver this message: if Rome (the Roman Empire) fell, so too could France and its (neocolonial) empire.

Emblematic of the classical style of the author, Beti's imperfect subjunctives, his allusions to Greek and Latin mythologies, and to the French Revolution create a challenging distance with his various readers. They can be interpreted as a (seriously playful) attempt on the writer's part to subvert the master's tongue by constantly shifting the dominant/subordinate position it hinges on. Evidencing the "rule," this African writer gains perceptible narrative control to prevent easy conclusions.

The Story of the Madman is easily summed up. It stages the rapid succession of dictatorial regimes in a fictitious African republic, during cocoa harvest, at the end of the 1980s.[6] With ironic verve, it marks the consequences of such a situation for the population, particularly for Chief Zoaételeu's village and for his two favorite sons, Zoaétoa and Narcisse. The narrative is loosely organized in nineteen unnumbered segments, which form the background of Zoaétoa's, the madman's evolution.

The novel's language is composed of two main registers, one more elevated than the other. Including words (such as "abjurations") that are challenging trademarks of the Cameroonian author, the more elevated register calls for an interpretive effort and has a rhetorical function. Occasionally resorting to the use of alliterations and to footnotes in which he provokes his readers into opening their dictionaries and in not taking "culture" for granted (see note p. 35), Beti testily communicates the Grand Guignol quality of political discourse as well as his engagement in representing it.

The second register sets the broad narrative landscape of *Madman* and is reminiscent of other Betian novels, such as the *Dzewatama* chronicle. *Madman,* however, makes more frequent and obvious use of narrative strategies inspired by African oral tradition, particularly the use of repetitions and of proverb-like sentences. In this book, repetitions give the narration a rhythm channeling the reader to heed the book's dominant trope: (dictatorial) power.

Since in *Madman* Latin is mostly the language of the political opponent to the dictatorship, a lawyer, and the author offers it without translation in the French version (although this English-language version does provide translations), it seems reasonable to talk about a process of encoding rather than a more straightforward act of quoting. This interpretation is confirmed when (and if) the reader answers the author's footnoted provocative urging and translates the "quotes" to find that they are predominantly excerpted from Virgil's *Aeneid,* Caesar's *Gallic Wars,* and Sallust's *Bellum Jugurthinum,* all texts about empire.

Latin is used, sparingly, by the narrator to comment on Narcisse's and the lawyer's behaviors. In the form of aphorisms, it punctuates Narcisse's shortcomings. In the form of commentaries, it underlines two contradictory notions at the core of Beti's representation of the lawyer-opponent. The first quote, "*Fit via vi* was his motto" (66), connotes the opponent's strength of character and decisiveness; the second mockingly casts doubt on his ability to be heard, and therefore on the relevance and effectiveness of his political message to the general population:

"'*Hannibal ad portas! Hannibal ad portas!*' they would shout in parody as soon as this cultured and perspicacious man entered a salon.

'Well, well, here comes the visionary!' a rival of the bar would comment in a low voice before greeting him with a thunderous, 'Greetings, new Cassandra.'" (129)

The lawyer is a complex representation. On the one hand, the character remains quite undeveloped: the lawyer-opponent has no name and is solely identified by his functions to defend and oppose. He has no personal life outside of his struggle for justice, and interestingly, his not having any love life is positively connoted as a proof of personal integrity. An idealist, he is a different model of a man.

On the other hand, the lawyer is a core character of *Madman,* and he illustrates values essential to the book. A Latinist and a champion of human rights, he is the author's double. But the inspired speeches of this political opponent, his very integrity and finesse, fail to mobilize the people who see him as somewhat of a . . . madman or, to use a term dear to Beti's heart, as a "dipsomaniac" of language. Trying to speak the truth of political oppression, forsaking a cheap populism, the lawyer is not understood. His "directive" remains "enigmatic" (150). A "Cassandra," the value of his speech resides in the denegation it elicits, and his "newness" (as in "new Cassandra" and "Cassandra of the shantytowns" (133, 136) fails to convince the reader of his radical difference from the famed archetype. In this respect, the figure of the lawyer-opponent meets that of the patriarch, Zoaételeu, whose grandiloquent and tentative discourse is compared to the pronouncements of an oracle. As is the case with Zoaételeu, the "truth" uttered by the lawyer remains suspended. It rises (the masses) but eventually dissolves into Latin "muttering" (156). It stays unintelligible.

In *Madman* the absence of social and political intelligence/intelligibility assumes the form of a general and systemic quid pro quo, experienced by all social classes, and again related to a form of madness. The lack of the author's translation for most of the Latin quotes constitutes a metaphor for the radical impossibility of oppositional political discourse. The exemplarity of the lawyer-opponent is again constructed as a paradox. Pitted against the hypocritical and blissfully ignorant behavior of his audience, it serves to illustrate that being exemplary does not make the militant an example.

Afterword

The second figure of the opponent to the dictatorial regime, "the English-speaking politician," is sketchily fashioned after John Fru N'Di, the leader of the SDF (Social Democratic Front) and Paul Biya's contender during the October 1992 presidential elections. Fru N'Di represented a political alternative when he launched his party in May 1990. His populist discourse appealed to the masses. Cameroon was then experiencing a period of hope, a rising of popular opinion, and an opening of the press and the radio—unfortunately later to be met by repression. In *Madman* the mastery lacking in the lawyer appears, at first, to be embodied in the "English-speaking guest," making him an alternative model for political leadership (201). In the long run, however, that model remains inoperative, and it disintegrates into a disappointing void.

Both the lawyer and the English-speaking guest manifest a moment in Beti's reflection on the state of oppositional politics in his country. While Rubenism still serves as a reference to the Cameroonian writer's ideology of literary resistance, it is not summoned as explicitly as it was in Beti's former novels. Beti's vision of the democratic culture he envisions for his country shows here, but it is blocked by the constant evocation of social morass and strongly put into question by Narcisse's and the lawyer's violent deaths, in the final scene. In this respect, *Madman* is more somber than Beti's preceding books. Verging at times on bitterness, it uses black humor to undercut easy signs of hope or naive idealism. Beti's sense of the historical mission he must fulfill, particularly toward younger generations of Cameroonians and Africans, is played out differently in this volume, in which the author strips his readers' illusions bare.

This is not to say that Beti's fighting spirit has abated or that his values have changed that much, but his living in the Cameroon and a more direct involvement in Cameroonian politics have influenced him anew. Beti's message remains revolutionary. *Madman* conveys that in the throes of dictatorship, when everything else has failed, there is a duty to revolt. The political philosophy emerging from the book typically, if more urgently, "prescribes a jealously independent conception of Africa and Africans" (Kom, "Mongo Beti: Théorie" 18). *Madman* offers a literary platform for the discussion of pressing historical problems, such as that of ethnicity. It illustrates Beti's resistance to essentialist definitions of ethnic differences, for example when the narrator (who is both critical and sympathetic) speaks of "national communities," and displays an inclusive understanding of the country, while the people in power talk of "ethnic groups" to try and divisively assert their authority (158, 81).

When, in the course of an interview I conducted with Mongo Beti in 1995 (reprinted below), I remarked to Beti that female characters remain scant and undeveloped in *Madman,* the author agreed with my assessment and indicated that realism had dictated this narrative construction of the feminine. *Madman*'s feminine landscape includes the usual, caricatural denunciation of the traditional woman's plight and of the "reproductive imperative" she lives under (Célérier 43). The novel typically represents gender roles and interactions critically and faults a patriarchal masculinity for the subjection of women.

Contrary to other books of Beti's however, *Madman* does not present any heroic female figures. Women remain secondary characters and are almost always portrayed as complacent under the yoke. The urban woman, Jeanne, Narcisse's "partner of the moment" (31), is a semi-prostitute, "more than ever faithful to her deplorable status" (37). Narcisse's unofficial bride, a young villager, does not have a name and is introduced as "the little fiancée imposed by Zoaételeu" (40). After she becomes pregnant by Narcisse (although some doubt is cast on who the father really is, and Zoaételeu, the quintessential paterfamilias, is held to be the other possible genitor), the imposed "little fiancée" is called "a monster" by the foreign nurses (91, 90). As for the narrator, he puts her in a category frequently reserved by Beti for village girls: that of the "pregnant adolescents" (91).

In *Madman,* as is the case in most novels by Beti, motherhood fails to give women status, but it is depicted even more caricaturally. The reader is again confronted with the Betian topos of the exploitative mother, selling her daughter to older men for her own financial profit and social advancement (see *Perpetua*). That practice is connoted slightly differently here however, since the exploitation cuts across class lines and affects the daughters of "privileged families" (113).

Contrary to *Lament for an African Pol,* for instance, the idea of filiation in *Madman* is exclusively tied to patriarchy. There are no positive relationships between women, and there is no matriarchal lineage. The discussion of the feminine is framed by that of the masculine. The text depicts a society where human relationships have become commodified and where prostitution is a modus vivendi. With the exception of the lawyer, all men exploit women. That love and what it may possibly mean is ironically and tentatively discussed constitutes a remarkable feature of this novel by Beti. But the discussion is repeatedly and systematically short-circuited by a depiction of sex as matter-of-fact or as a means to an end, an act always dissociated from emotions.

Some of Narcisse's actions lead the reader to believe that he may offer a different masculine model. Indeed, Narcisse appears at first to distance himself from his father's traditional vision of a man. Talking to Zoaételeu, who wants to see him perpetuate their family with the village girl he has chosen, Narcisse vehemently rejects the old chief's proposal: "'If you are trying to get me to mate with an ugly woman so that you can have more grandchildren, Father, that's crazy,' he flared. 'Where does anybody come off praising a woman just because she has wide hips that bode well for pregnancies?'" (11). But Narcisse, for his education and fortuitous insights, proves himself to be too weak to break the mold. Lethargic and self-serving, he ends up following the parasitic pattern played out by other young urban men around him. A generic "elegant delinquent of indefinite status" (43), he lives off Jeanne's wealthier occasional lovers and makes no real efforts to take charge of his own existence.

The first passage of *Madman* in which Jeanne and Narcisse

are in the village is interesting, since Narcisse's extreme laziness and Jeanne's activity indirectly translate Beti's conviction about "the destitution, if not the cultural sterility, of the masculine function in this society" and the central role of women, "pillars of the village" (*La France contre l'Afrique* 18). In the same line of thought, Narcisse conveys another underlying theme in the writer's work: men's boastful obsession with reproduction and their concomitant and paradoxical abandonment of their paternal responsibilities.

Beti's elaboration of the feminine in *The Story of the Madman* recalls that of Perpétue in *Perpetua and the Habit of Unhappiness* and of Agathe in the *Dzewatama* chronicle. Womanhood is shrouded in similar silence and oppression. What departs from Beti's earlier characterizations of women, particularly of working-class urban women, is the writer's insistence on the fact of prostitution in their lives. This echoes the impressions cynically related by the writer when he came back to his country in 1994: "Today, in the city, the only hope for work for a young working-class girl, aged fifteen to twenty, is prostitution. Those, and they are quite numerous, who do not resign themselves to this situation come back to the village" (*La France contre l'Afrique* 21).

To sum up this brief analysis of Beti's construction of the feminine in *Madman*, one can say that Beti is consistent with what he said to E. Brière in a 1977 interview: "I am politically a feminist, . . . [but] I am also a realist writer . . . , so [in my work] there are inevitably women who are objectified" (73). Beti portrays women's oppression as well as some of the ways in which it is socially compounded. The problem with his characterization of the feminine in *Madman*, however, is that it is not sufficiently developed to ground and substantiate his implicit denunciation.

There is a thematic link in Beti's novels between a lethal masculinity, alcohol, fratricide, and madness. Portrayed as radically divorced from others, men like Zoaétoa, who fooled themselves into believing in power, stagger in their isolation. Each of them is directly and indirectly responsible for their sibling's early death. "No longer at ease," they have lost awareness and humanity: "Captain Zoaétoa, officer in the special commando corps . . . son of Zoaételeu, noble offspring of the illustrious lineage of Zambo Menduga and of men each more valorous than the last, will doubtless rot in the midst of the refuse where he rummaged for his miserable sustenance, and passersby will hold their noses without so much as a backward glance for what they will take to be the carrion of some wandering animal" (162).

Emblematic of the story we are told here, madness is far from being a readily understood symbol of neocolonial alienation. Since the topos of madness is intrinsic to French-speaking African literatures, *The Story of the Madman* has a plot circumscribable not merely to that character's narrative "life" but to a literary tradition. This picture of a "madman" is rooted in a syncretic understanding of what madness may signify, as each reader comes to the concept with his or her own cultural definition and mediates the picture of madness drawn by the writer.

This novel's madness sanctions a collective national condition. The madness of Zoaétoa, the "naked man," is his father's madness as it is their people's. That (criminal) confusion has its roots in a botched "independence" that the late Nigerian Ogoni writer Ken Saro Wiwa described as internal colonization, and that the narrator of *Madman* conveys as follows: "It is also true that the spiral of fury and madness triggered by independence created an inhuman climate that precious few were able to resist. The population of madmen that haunts the streets of our cities and who all have tragic stories similar to this one bears witness to that fact" (57).

To conclude, let us say that through the intricate fable entitled *The Story of the Madman,* Mongo Beti pointedly moves his readers to consider the personal and collective consequences of the painful chaos brought about by a "scornful decolonization" (*Main basse* 146). And he calls on his compatriots to care for the soul of their country.

Interview with Mongo Beti
by Patricia-Pia Célérier

The following interview was conducted in August 1995 at Beti's then-new bookstore, the Librairie des Peuples Noirs, in the Quartier Tsinga of Yaoundé, Cameroon, and in the presence of Odile Tobner.[7]

P.P.C.: Could you explain your creative approach in *The Story of the Madman?*

M.B.: *The Story of the Madman* constantly questions the probability of the narration. It illustrates the problematics of the postcolonial state and of a people whose values are disintegrating, who are engulfed in fantasies and never sure of reality. The one-party state takes over by promising a semblance of structure and more material goods. This system deploys itself in a so-called francophone space, whose main characteristic is an absence of dialogue.

P.P.C.: In *The Story of the Madman,* does the figure of John Fru N'Di, President Paul Biya's opponent during the 1992 presidential elections, replace that of the Cameroonian patriot, Ruben Um Nyobè, who is omnipresent in the rest of your work? Do you need a militant and nationalist character in your novels?

M.B.: I seem to be needing one, since this character is recurrent. Cameroonians expect a liberator, someone who can begin to provide them with an explanation.

P.P.C.: Does this correspond to a need for a model or to the awaiting of a messiah?

M.B.: There is a messianic expectation at the root of the population's aspirations. Nobody believes in the constraints of daily militantism anymore. We dream of a magical figure who will rescue us and take us to the Promised Land. I was still in high school when a formidable enthusiasm for Um Nyobè welled up. Through him, we were able to transcend temporarily the divisions, tribal and others, of our society. Since his death, the Cameroonian collective unconscious has been waiting for a second Um.

P.P.C.: A conspiratorial atmosphere prevails in your work. Why?

M.B.: This may call for a psychoanalytic analysis. . . . For a long time, I dreamt of an underground threat. I also love detective novels, those of George Simenon, Agatha Christie, and Chester Himes, whom I particularly appreciate because of his picturesque sense of humor and the way he renders the reality of Harlem.

P.P.C.: In *The Story of the Madman,* what does the repetition of the phrase "Let us wait for the year 2000" mean?

M.B.: It is neither prophetic nor millenarian. The lawyer is a man who can see far, a visionary, not a mystic. He knows that Africa is going to change, liberate itself, and he proclaims it. He also knows that this emancipation will not come easily. "Let us wait for the year 2000" is a striking formula that uses the approaching millennium. It is an easy formula for this character, who is something of a poet and who has a sense of the power of the word.

P.P.C.: You successively construct the lawyer as a noble Roman warrior and as a French revolutionary hero, a Saint-Just. This characterization is not original to *The Story of the Madman.* El Malek, the political opponent in *Les deux mères de Guillaume Ismaël Dzewatama,* is himself compared with a Roman warrior and has virtues modeled after French revolutionary figures.

M.B.: A person of French culture does not have hundreds of different ways to portray a hero. Saint-Just is a terrible and extraordinary figure. He has a place in my personal pantheon. I am also a Latinist, and references to Latin culture come naturally to me.

P.P.C.: In *The Story of the Madman,* there is a provocative discussion about "le lettrisme" and "les lettrés" [scholars]. What do you mean by that?

M.B.: It is not an elitist but a sociological vision of culture. "Le lettrisme" is a classification that applies to Cameroon. It designates people expecting to be granted a degree without studying, such as some in power here who are frequently half ignorant and whose status as scholars is certified only by a display of senseless and empty diplomas. As for me, I think that education, critical judgment, and awareness determine understanding and, consequently, the type of actions to be undertaken.

P.P.C.: *The Story of the Madman* greatly relies on visual imagery. It attempts to reproduce chaos, through a number of graphic repetitions, for instance. Can you comment on this?

M.B.: For someone wanting to be understood by the people and to strike the imagination, there is nothing more expressive than visual images. I may not have been conscious that using the means of literature, I approached the cinematic techniques of close-up, overall shot, and panning. I am influenced by the films most accessible to a nonspecialist, John Ford's westerns for example. *The Battleship Potemkin* [by Sergey Eisenstein] shows close-ups of soldiers' boots, and this image is enough to convey an impression of brutality. In our villages, this is what you see when the soldiers arrive. The alignment of these shoes symbolizes repression.

P.P.C.: How do you explain the growing importance of the media in your work?

M.B.: The Biya system does not aim at informing people but rather at making them believe something. To that effect, people are told lies. In the context of a weakened dictatorship, the press has become an instrument for change. It informs. It opens its readers to outside opinions, and that means a lot.

P.P.C.: Why is the idea of civil war recurrent in your work?

M.B.: We live in an atmosphere of latent civil war. In 1991, the Cameroonian authorities supplied the Betis with weapons.

The universities, built for ten thousand people were accommodating forty thousand, and the country was experiencing a real May 1968, but limited to the campuses. When the army came on campus, it chased the revolutionary students, and the armed population helped by rounding them up. No investigation was ever conducted, and the government made no public comment. Some journalists, like Pius Njawé, from *Le Messager,* did investigate though, and they know the facts. In Cameroon, there are provinces where the police cannot go, in the far North, for example. The government calls this phenomenon "roadblockers" or "tribal war between Aratchawas and Bororos." In reality, the situation clearly demonstrates the state's systematic refusal to engage in dialogue with the opposition.

P.P.C.: Can you explain your perception of the relationship between history and literature?

M.B.: I do not see how a Cameroonian can write and not testify against the oppression of his people. This literary process is no luxury. You cannot compare it to that of a twentieth-century French writer at work on a historical novel. A committed approach to writing is, for most of us Africans, a necessity, and the plot of my novels is not a mere stroke of luck.

P.P.C.: Which writers and books have influenced you the most?

M.B.: *Uncle Tom's Cabin* by Harriet Beecher Stowe is the novel that has inspired me the most. Professor Guyon, from the faculty of Aix-en-Provence, taught me to love Balzac. Victor Hugo, the novelist and prose writer, amazed me by his virtuosity and the prolific quality of his literary production. Our colonial education offered some models, among which were *Les orientales, Hernani, Les misérables.* As a teenager, I liked *The Pickwick Papers* by Dickens. I discovered Voltaire while teaching. The explosive charge of *Candide* and even that of *L'ingénu* pleased me. I also liked *Toussaint Louverture* by Aimé Césaire, and the novels of Richard Wright.

P.P.C.: Other African writers, notably those of a younger generation, claim that writing a novel has more to do with aesthetics than with historical "reality." Their commitment is expressed differently from yours.

M.B.: There is not just one definition for the novel, but aesthetic commitments remain the prerogative of a minority. Considering current politics, it is vital to move away from ambitious and opportunistic preoccupations. The real issue is the status the writer assumes in a society. The themes of my books are eminently popular: evangelization, the peasant going to the city, the schoolboy coming back home, rediscovering his habits and beliefs. . . . The character of Perpétue represents the African woman, facing situations her education had not prepared her for: the city, a polygamous husband, and adultery. It is not adultery as a subject that is new, but the circumstances of the adultery.

P.P.C.: You insist that your novels answer to an imperative for truth.

M.B.: I am not the only one to say that. Other writers, including my friend the Congolese writer Tchichellé Tchivéla, are of this opinion. And Tchivéla's short stories generate the same kind of relationship with the French government.

P.P.C.: But how can a novel, an imaginary creation, appeal to truth?

M.B.: The issue is not whether or not it is imaginary, but how the authorities react in the face of this imaginary creation, if they recognize it. *Madame Bovary* is an imaginary creation, nevertheless Napoleon III's government recognized itself in Flaubert's satire of its morals.

P.P.C.: Young African and Caribbean writers are increasingly using Creole or Pidgin in their works.

M.B.: Yes, but I did so in [*Remember*] *Ruben* because I absolutely wanted to characterize a neighborhood of Douala called Congo, where the movement was born.

Afterword

P.P.C.: Does this type of work with language interest you?

M.B.: It would interest me more if I were a dramatist. It is not possible to make an old African peasant speak French on a stage.

P.P.C.: It has been said that French-speaking African writers using the imperfect subjunctive stick to criteria of excellence that should be reconsidered.

M.B.: I have nothing against this trend. However, Hugo, a great popular writer, used the imperfect subjunctive in the nineteenth century, when three out of every four French persons were illiterate. Most Bretons, Basques, and Alsatians spoke only the languages of their regions. In my opinion, this issue hinges on specific and contextual circumstances.

P.P.C.: It also depends on the degree of cultural intermixing within the society.

M.B.: To break down a language, one needs a model. What would result from the breaking down of the French language in a country such as Cameroon, where 120 different languages coexist? West Indians, on the other hand, have another possible model, since Creole is almost a national language.

P.P.C.: But should "classic French" be systematically destabilized for the supremacist construction of a "francophonie" to become undone, for instance?

M.B.: Creating a linguistic model that is accessible to the people, not only to Cameroonians, but to Africans, seems to me more important. One does not change a language any which way. Du Bellay changed French, in *Défense et illustration de la langue française,* but by conceiving of new rules. If you do not do that, anarchy sets in, and anarchy means obscurantism. French represents for us Africans the possibility of communication between people of different cultures and languages.

P.P.C.: But French itself is not a stable language.

Afterword

M.B.: Changes occurring at the periphery are set in action around the center, the existing core. If we consider jazz, the twelve-beat blues had to be done away with, at a certain point, so as to open the music up to something else. However, any jazz musician is conscious that he must know how to play the blues, Charlie Parker, the great jazz revolutionary, included. Making a revolution implies the conservation and the survival of a means of communication, which language is. The raw material of art is communication. I am speaking now both as a teacher of French literature and as a writer: when I write, I want to be understood by as many people as possible.

P.P.C.: What responses do you hope to generate in your readers?

M.B.: First and foremost, a reflection about the Black condition, then a curiosity about Africa, and pleasure derived from the originality of the narrative situation and of the characters.

That we had to go to Europe in order to write and publish does not mean we want to address Europeans first. I always quote these words by Stendhal: "I shall be read fifty years from now." I write thinking of the legacy I will be leaving to the next generation of Africans.

P.P.C.: What is the book that was the most pleasing for you to write?

M.B.: *Le pauvre Christ de Bomba* because it revealed me to myself. When I wrote *Ville cruelle,* I was highly influenced by Richard Wright's *Native Son,* the plot and inspiration of which I admired. In *Le pauvre Christ de Bomba,* I intended to demystify the missionary in the colonies, and I jumped into it without knowing where I was going. I invented the form, the content, and that is when I found my way.

P.P.C.: What are your work habits?

M.B.: In order to write, I must reflect a long time. My intention must be very precise. *The End of the Affair,* by Graham Greene, portrays a writer who every morning forces

Afterword

himself to write a certain number of pages. That, in my opinion, is a good method. I personally do not make any outline. Having thought it out, I develop an idea of the action scheme (the exposition, the story line, the dramatic turn of events, and the dénouement). I proceed by creating each situation and by articulating its importance. Generally speaking, I write a fifty-page first draft, then come up with a definite version. When I am warmed up, I can write ten pages a day. I wrote *Perpétue* during a two-month school holiday in 1973. Yet, doing nothing but writing would bore me immensely. An African intellectual, I live through ideas, but I like action and have varied interests.

P.P.C.: Did the stories your mother used to tell you at night, in the village, make you a writer?

M.B.: Oh yes! The telling of tales is the only literary training my traditional background provided me with. All the kids who participate in the clan's evening gatherings use it. It is extremely educative because each one must tell a story, the adults first, and then the children. The first time I was told it would be my turn, my mother, knowing I was shy, spent all day teaching me how to tell a story, how to insist on one thing or the other so as not to frustrate the listeners. She instructed me on how to pace my narration and hold the audience's attention. Later on, a critic remarked that I did not know how to give depth to a character and that, consequently, I was more of a storyteller than a novelist. My mother had already drawn my attention to this, when I was a child. She had taught me the art of preparation and emphasis, the art of flashback, that gets people interested.

P.P.C.: You went from oral literature to written literature, in a language that was not your mother tongue.

M.B.: Yes, the African child's relationship to French is curious. When I was growing up, children were immersed in this language very young. There was no radio and no television. The colonizer was French, and if you wanted to be well considered, you had to speak his language.

P.P.C.: You went to school in Mbalmayo?

M.B.: Yes, but I began my schooling in the village, at the missionaries' primary school, where I stayed for one year. At that time, if the teachers caught you speaking your mother tongue, in my case Ewondo, they made you wear a dunce cap. To get rid of it, you had to pass it on to one of your classmates, so the pupils would spy on each other to determine who was speaking in the native language. The one with the cap at the end of the day was fined, very little, but that was enough to create a certain atmosphere.

P.P.C.: In *The Story of the Madman,* female characters remain undeveloped narratively. Why is this, especially since heroic female figures appear in your previous novels?

M.B.: I do not know, and it is indeed a question for a critic to examine. When I consider the political actors in the Cameroon, I do not see women. My more or less conscious elaboration of the context for *The Story of the Madman* follows my observation of Cameroonian society and that of a political landscape where only men—military men, patriarchs, or lawyers—are at the forefront. For the majority of women in this country, there is no other solution than prostitution. In *The Story of the Madman,* in addition to Narcisse's friend who is a prostitute, I created a caricatural figure of the traditional woman, a woman who is burdened with children, goes to the fields, does the cooking, but remains unacknowledged by the rest of the world. This may be an inaccurate vision.

P.P.C.: What meaning do you attach to the use of your different pseudonyms?

M.B.: As far as my first pseudonym, Eza Boto, is concerned, I needed to cover my tracks. An Anglicist friend, in Aix-en-Provence, used to talk to me about Ezra Pound, and I was obsessed with the consonance of these two words. My family name, Biyidi, is impossible to spell out, and I needed a Bantu-sounding pen name. I randomly chose Eza Boto. However, this choice leaves the door open to all kinds of comments, since in Ewondo, "Eza" means "other," "of the others," and "Boto" is a rather common word for "man."

P.P.C.: Why did you abandon that pseudonym, Eza Boto, "the other man"?

M.B.: The book had been poorly launched by Présence Africaine, and I had a falling out with them. I wanted my next novel, *Le pauvre Christ de Bomba,* to be published by a large publishing company. Laffont accepted it, and I chose my current pseudonym, Mongo Beti, or "the child from the homeland."

P.P.C.: Were you afraid of losing your readership when you abandoned your first pseudonym?

M.B.: I had few readers at that time. When *Ville cruelle* was published, it went unnoticed, and it remained unknown for a long time. Only when UNESCO, which was financing French-speaking universities, demanded that local writers be included in high school and university curricula, were 400,000 copies of *Ville cruelle* sold.

P.P.C.: In your opinion, why do your books about the colonial period tend to be included in the curriculum in Africa, and not those about independence?

M.B.: Since independence, I have the profile of the opponent. My books on the colonial period are deemed neutral, whereas those written after this period are rejected. But not all my novels about the colonial period have remained in the curriculum, because education is extremely politicized here. As it is, *Le pauvre Christ* has been taken out.

P.P.C.: Since you came back to live in Cameroon, you have commented on political events essentially by means of newspaper articles—in *Le Messager* and *Génération,* for instance. Is the political essay—and some have called your essays satirical "pamphlets"—a literary form you will no longer practice because it was mostly appropriate to exile?

M.B.: The term pamphlet is often used pejoratively. It implies that the author is biased and has produced a hasty and minimal effort in writing the piece in question. It suggests that he has cheated with reality. *Le Monde Diplomatique* called *Main basse sur le Cameroon* a satirical pamphlet, and I objected to this term because *Main basse* has more to do with investigative journalism. There is nothing in this book that is untrue or unverifiable, except maybe for a few speculations on the circumstances under which [Ernest] Ouandié was betrayed. That is why Cameroonians are attached to *Main basse* and why [President Georges] Pompidou ordered its confiscation. It is true that I express opinions and stand emphatically against state power, but then we would have to consider *Le rouge et le noir,* which is a politically committed novel, a satirical pamphlet.

P.P.C.: What about the future?

M.B.: I am working on a novel, and when I am mobilized by an idea, I concentrate on it.[8] I am very involved in my village, where I dedicate myself to the development of a form of agriculture beyond mere subsistence. We grow corn, tomatoes, plantain, sugarcane, etc., on several acres and sell our products in the city. I dig wells and will soon open up a school.

Notes

My gratitude to K. Chukwu and to Professors A. Kom, C. Reno, K. Robertson, E. Schneider, and T. Spear.

1. Beti's father had died when Beti was seven years old.
2. Interview with PPC.
3. Ouandié was executed on 19 January 1971.
4. All subsequent quotes from Beti's *Stronghold on the Cameroon* and *France against Africa* from A. Kom and E. Brière's articles published in *Présence Francophone* and from PPC's article in *Notre Librairie* were translated by PPC.
5. I am using the term *ex-colonies* for argument's sake. Cameroon

Afterword

was really under the "trusteeship" of the French government until 1957.

6. As in *Ville cruelle.*

7. The interview was made possible by the Vassar College Mellon Fund.

8. *Trop de soleil tue l'amour* (1999).

Bibliography

Novels by Mongo Beti

Beti, Mongo. *Ville cruelle*. 2d edition. Paris: Présence Africaine, 1971.

———. *Le pauvre Christ de Bomba*. 2d edition. Paris: Laffont, 1976. Trans. by Gerald Moore, *The Poor Christ of Bomba*. London: Heinemann, 1971.

———. *Mission terminée*. Paris: Buchet-Chastel, 1957. Trans. by Peter Green, *Mission to Xala*. London: Heinemann, 1964.

———. *Le roi miraculé*. Paris: Buchet-Chastel, 1958. Trans. by Peter Green, *King Lazarus*. London: Heinemann, 1960.

———. *Perpétue et l'habitude du malheur*. Paris: Buchet-Chastel, 1974. Trans. by John Reed and Clive Wake, *Perpetua and the Habit of Unhappiness*. London: Heinemann, 1978.

———. *Remember Ruben*. 2d edition. Paris: 10/18, 1974. Trans. by Gerald Moore, *Remember Ruben*. London: Heinemann, 1980.

———. *La ruine presque cocasse d'un polichinelle: Remember Ruben II*. Paris: Peuples Noirs, 1979. Trans. by Richard Bjornson, *Lament for an African Pol*. Boulder: Three Continents, 1985.

———. *Les deux mères de Guillaume Ismaël Dzewatama, Futur camionneur*. Paris: Buchet-Chastel, 1983.

———. *La revanche de Guillaume Ismaël Dzewatama*. Paris: Buchet-Chastel, 1984.

———. *L'histoire du fou*. Paris: Julliard, 1994.

———. *Trop de soleil tue l'amour*. Paris: Julliard, 1999.
———. *Branle-bas en noir et blanc*. Paris: Julliard, 2000.

Essays by Mongo Beti

Beti, Mongo. "Afrique Noire, littérature rose." *Présence Africaine* 1 (1955).
———. *Main basse sur le Cameroon: Autopsie d'une décolonisation*. 3d edition. Rouen: Peuples Noirs, 1984.
———. *Lettre ouverte aux Camerounais ou la deuxième mort de Ruben Um Nyobè*. Paris: Peuples Noirs, 1986.
———, and Odile Tobner. *Dictionnaire de la Négritude*. Paris: L'Harmattan, 1989.
———. *La France contre L'Afrique: Retour au Cameroun*. Paris: La Découverte, 1993.

Select Bibliography on Mongo Beti

Arnold, Stephen H., ed. *Critical Perspectives on Mongo Beti*. Boulder: Lynne Rienner, 1998.
Battestini, M., and R. Mercier, eds. *Mongo Beti, ecrivain camerounais*. Paris: Nathan, 1964.
Bjornson, Richard. *The African Quest for Freedom and Identity: Cameroonian Writing and the National Experience*. Bloomington: Indiana UP, 1991.
Brière, Eloïse. "Mutisme et prise de parole: Le personnage féminin chez Mongo Beti." *Présence Francophone* 42 (1993): 73-87.
Célérier, Patricia-Pia. "Mongo Beti: Regard sur la maternité." *Notre Librairie* 117 (1994): 39-43.
Davey, John. *Mission to Kala*. London: Heinemann, 1977.
Fame Ndongo, Jacques. *L'esthétique romanesque de Mongo Beti: Essai sur les sources traditionnelles de l'écriture moderne en Afrique*. Paris: Présence Africaine, 1985.
Jacquey, Marie-Clotilde, and Ambroise Kom, eds. *Littérature Camerounaise I. Notre Librairie* 99 (1989).

Bibliography

Jacquey, Marie-Clodilde, and Ambroise Kom, eds. *Littérature Camerounaise II. Notre Librairie* 100 (1990).

Kom, Ambroise. "Mongo Beti: Théorie et pratique de l'écriture en Afrique Noire francophone." *Présence Francophone* 42 (1993): 11-24.

Kom, Ambroise, ed. *Mongo Beti: 40 ans d'écriture, 60 ans de dissidence. Présence Francophone* 42 (special issue; 1993).

Kom, Ambroise, and Christian Petr, eds. *La littérature au Cameroun. Europe* 774 (1993).

Mbock, Charly-Gabriel. *Comprendre "Ville cruelle."* Issy-les-Moulineaux: Saint-Paul, 1981.

Melone, Thomas. *Mongo Beti: L'homme et le destin.* Paris: Présence Africaine, 1971.

Mouralis, Bernard. *Comprendre l'oeuvre de Mongo Beti.* Issy-les-Moulineaux, 1981.

CARAF Books
Caribbean and African Literature
Translated from French

A number of writers from very different cultures in Africa and the Caribbean continue to write in French although their daily communication may be in another language. While this use of French brings their creative vision to a more diverse international public, it inevitably enriches and often deforms the conventions of classical French, producing new regional idioms worthy of notice in their own right. The works of these francophone writers offer valuable insights into a highly varied group of complex and evolving cultures. The CARAF Books series was founded in an effort to make these works available to a public of English-speaking readers.

For students, scholars, and general readers, CARAF offers selected novels, short stories, plays, poetry, and essays that have attracted attention across national boundaries. In most cases the works are published in English for the first time. The specialists presenting the works have often interviewed the author in preparing background materials, and each title includes an original essay situating the work within its own literary and social context and offering a guide to thoughtful reading.

CARAF Books

Guillaume Oyônô-Mbia
and Seydou Badian
Faces of African Independence:
Three Plays
Translated by Clive Wake

Olympe Bhêly-Quénum
Snares without End
Translated by Dorothy S. Blair

Bertène Juminer
The Bastards
Translated by Keith Q. Warner

Tchicaya U Tam'Si
The Madman and the Medusa
Translated by Sonja Haussmann
Smith and William Jay Smith

Alioum Fantouré
Tropical Circle
Translated by Dorothy S. Blair

Edouard Glissant
Caribbean Discourse:
Selected Essays
Translated by J. Michael Dash

Daniel Maximin
Lone Sun
Translated by Nidra Poller

Aimé Césaire
Lyric and Dramatic Poetry, 1946–82
Translated by Clayton Eshleman
and Annette Smith

René Depestre
The Festival of the Greasy Pole
Translated by Carrol F. Coates

Kateb Yacine
Nedjma
Translated by Richard Howard

Léopold Sédar Senghor
The Collected Poetry
Translated by Melvin Dixon

Maryse Condé
I, Tituba, Black Witch of Salem
Translated by Richard Philcox

Assia Djebar
*Women of Algiers in
Their Apartment*
Translated by Marjolijn de Jager

Dany Bébel-Gisler
*Leonora: The Buried Story
of Guadeloupe*
Translated by Andrea Leskes

Lilas Desquiron
Reflections of Loko Miwa
Translated by Robin Orr Bodkin

Jacques Stephen Alexis
General Sun, My Brother
Translated by Carrol F. Coates

Malika Mokeddem
Of Dreams and Assassins
Translated by K. Melissa Marcus

Werewere Liking
It Shall Be of Jasper and Coral and
Love-across-a-Hundred-Lives
Translated by Marjolijn de Jager

Ahmadou Kourouma
*Waiting for the Vote
of the Wild Animals*
Translated by Carrol F. Coates

Mongo Beti
The Story of the Madman
Translated by Elizabeth Darnel